MOTHER'S INSTINCT

By
GD Jackman

This book is copyright GD Jackman 2019

No part may be copied in any form whatsoever without the written permission of the author.

This book is a work of fiction any resemblance to persons, living or deceased, is entirely coincidental

This book is dedicated to my mum. She always said I should write something and now I have.
Thanks Mum.

Contents

Prologue 1

Chapter One 4

Chapter Two 8

Chapter Three 16

Chapter Four 25

Chapter Five 38

Chapter Six 42

Chapter Seven 47

Chapter Eight 49

Chapter Nine 54

Chapter Ten 58

Chapter Eleven 61

Chapter Twelve 66

Chapter Thirteen 72

Chapter Fourteen 79

Chapter Sixteen 93

Chapter Seventeen 95

Chapter Eighteen 99

Chapter Nineteen 105

Chapter Twenty 110

Chapter Twenty-Two 124
Chapter Twenty-Three 131
Chapter Twenty-Five 138
Chapter Twenty-Six 142
Chapter Twenty-Seven 148
Chapter Twenty-Eight 159
Chapter Twenty-Nine 164
Chapter Thirty 165
Chapter Thirty-One 170
Chapter Thirty-Two 175

Prologue

Instinct: *an involuntary prompting to action.*

The crowded train slid to a smooth halt. As the doors swished open, she was the first one to pass, careful not to lose a loose shoe down the gap between the platform and the step. The sound of footsteps, loud ones, clicking ones, and slow ones all joined in with her own as the relieved passengers alighted from the hot train. She made her way slowly along the busy platform and tried to blend in, head bowed a little so that the new hairstyle fell across her face and pulled the long black overcoat a little tighter. She felt uncomfortable in the noisy surroundings, exposed, as if all eyes were on her – they weren't – she'd checked, but it was an eerie feeling. Her head itched, the nylon weave scratching her. She put the ticket in the machine and paused...when the green light came on she relaxed and walked on through the barrier...waited for alarm bells to go off ...they didn't...she sighed deeply, then, holding her breath, quickly scanned her eyes around in case someone had heard...No. She breathed out and pushed forward into the crowd. Then she froze. A shout from behind was immediately followed by a strong hand on her shoulder.

'Excuse me ...Miss...' Hot breath crossed her ear, moving the thick, curly hair. Please no…NO. She tensed as the man came around to face her.

'You dropped this?' The man panted, holding patterned cloth towards her. The sweat must have shown on her face. 'Are you...erm, okay, do you need to sit down?' He peered at her...too closely...she knew she seemed rude as she grabbed at the scarf he held out. She brushed him aside, a quick 'thanks', over her shoulder appeased her conscience. As she rushed away, she stuffed the soft material deep into her pocket. Felt the cold, hard metal of the knife that waited there. She exited the station, the sudden sunlight hurting her eyes then she was carried away in the crowd of the busy, bustling the street. A voice deep within her shouted that she was doing the right thing...even though it was wrong. *Very wrong.*

Part One

The Early Years

Chapter One

1979

'Twin girls! how lovely. You'll certainly have your hands full there. Still, at least Dan has a good business going here.' Mona looked at the girls. She knew what Lucy had gone through to get them but still managed to sound a little put out.

Lucy pushed up the sleeves of her thin white cardigan and shook her head, her wavy blonde hair swayed and caught the low afternoon sun causing a golden halo around her. She knew her sister envied her marriage and now, it seemed, her children. She carefully worded her reply.

'Your Phil's got you a decent life.' She replied evenly. Married to Dan's older brother Mona was not too badly off herself. He had a good job at the local builder's merchant and he repaired and sold bicycles from their shed. Lucy was not prepared to let Mona go through the usual routine of whinging again. Their parents really must have known something when they christened *her*! 'And we *will* need money, looking at how much they are managing to put away to wet the baby's heads. They've had enough to drown themselves...and half the village besides.' Lucy tutted good naturedly and gazed back down at the two plump, pink girls. Along with all mothers, she had such hopes for them. They carried one each upstairs, out of the way, as the party was now getting louder by the minute. In the bedroom, after they had lain them in the matching pink lacy cots, another joint effort as Dan had made the frames and she the mattress and quilt sets, Lucy pulled up straight and give her sister an understanding look, then she covered the girls with a white cotton sheet, made sure the mobiles above were turning and that they had a watchful teddy on the end of each cot as they settled down. The mothering instinct stronger now, she laid a sympathetic hand on her siblings' shoulder and gently said, 'Don't worry, it *will* happen for you too. Look how many times I've tried.' Lucy recalled the several miscarriages before these two and, if the "family curse" was to be believed, she would probably have several more. 'Let's join the others.' Lucy turned away towards the door but Mona lingered. As she stroked their faces she looked up, eyes full of sadness.

'I don't know how you can bear to be parted from them.'

In the farm garden Lucy watched her husband. It had been a long day and the auburn stubble now appearing on his face caught the light as he dad danced with his brother, hands and arms waving up and down, the beer bottle in one of them spitting its contents over anyone who got too close, there were few, most were sitting around chatting and eating, or dancing, well away from the two drunken men who were, it seemed, in a complete and happy world of their own. She knew he wouldn't be seen sober again today and that tomorrow he would be skulking around, keeping out of the way as he nursed a murderous hangover and wondering out loud, to all within earshot, why couldn't he shake this mysterious headache. They would all just smile at him and suggest aspirin. It was nothing that some fresh air wouldn't sort out though. They were so lucky in many ways she knew. Dan was tall with dark, chestnut hair, she with her blonde hair and waiflike stature. She was stronger than she looked though. He worked hard for his family. Too hard sometimes but he always shrugged it off and honestly, she knew he was happiest outside, he often said he couldn't wait for some helpers around the place and looked at her with that way of his that made her feel, even now, like a shy schoolgirl and the comfortable arms he would wrap around her. The perfect fit. Now they had the girls and she just knew they would grow up beautiful. Blessed. She looked around the yard, twilight was coming and the strings of multicoloured lights, the haybales for seats and clean lemon tablecloths, made from old bedsheets, on the make shift table; planks and a couple of sheep pens. It was lovely to see her family, and friends, here. The enforced move to the outskirts of the next village for the farm, although perfect for them, had made her feel quite lonely to start with and despite the tranquillity, or maybe because of it, their home village seemed a world away. In reality, she could walk it in half an hour.

Today was a double celebration as Dan's senior farm hand, Reg, had decided, with some gentle nudging, to retire. She laughed at the thought of that, she just *knew* he would still be spending nearly all his time here anyway. He was a widower now and had taken to coming to dinner every Tuesday evening and again for Sunday lunch. They had both assured him it needn't stop. Lucy liked Reg, with his snow-white hair, split by the yellow streak from years of smoking, though they didn't seem to have harmed him much, still strong enough to throw the sheep around, but he really *was* too old and Dan had been doing most of the work anyway. But, without Reg, they wouldn't have been as settled and happy as they'd become. Lucy stopped short when, in a sudden lull, she heard Dan's voice proclaiming that "he needed a son next". She pulled a face. Just let him come near her for a while! She peered out of the kitchen window and took in the lush green land, the promise of the summer just around the corner and knew how lucky she was. It wasn't always that way though and, she supposed, it would always be up and down, normal life was just like that, she paused, yes, she mused, finally she *did* have a normal family life. She made two cups of tea and, handing one to Mona, they went, arm in arm, back out to the party.

Chapter Two

'Nearly there.' Dan and Lucy bounced along the dirt track, in his little white van, between the barren fields in mid Sussex, for what seemed like an eternity, in fact it was about ten minutes but the excitement between them was building with each bump.

'Dan if you are not careful this little one is going to arrive right now!' Lucy cradled the large round bump under her cotton dress, covered in tiny flowers. She had made it herself including a let-out waist to accommodate the growth of her stomach. Blonde tendrils escaped the loose pony tail and her hand wiped them, irritably, away from her eyes but she quickly resumed her tight grip on the door as a huge pot hole appeared ahead. Dan skilfully avoided it, and turned the last bend.

'There it is.' In the distance a house loomed dark and lonely. From the drive it looked like it was stuck, out of place on top of the hill, a bit of an afterthought. As they arrived nearer, another slope came into view behind to afford some protection at the back. From the front it gazed over land that was flat *and* sloping.

'How are you going to work that!' Lucy was disappointed. She had expected lots of flat green fields with plenty of scope for planting.

'No problem,' he paused, let out a long slow breath and continued, 'with sheep.' He looked into her eyes, willing her to believe in him, in them, together, she knew he felt, they were invincible.

'Sheep!' Lucy's eyes widened and she stared at him, the disbelief obvious on her face. 'But you don't...'

'It's alright I have a man.' He continued quickly. 'His name's Reg, he *is* a bit old but...' Lucy wasn't listening or even looking at him anymore. She was staring towards the farmhouse. She heaved herself out of the van and walked slowly, with some difficulty, taking it all in. The open land in front, more dusty compacted mud than grass, this surrounded by a waist high drystone wall, missing large sections. The grass covered mounds in front of it probably hid most of the rocks that had fallen off. The original five bar gate, now just three or four pieces, laying useless on the ground, weeds growing through it. The posts that had held it in place long ago rotted away, the remaining pieces making homes for all sorts of crawling creatures. Her eyes lifted to the large, square building, built for practicality, nothing fancy here. Flat, rotten frames surrounding dark, grimy windows, some broken, paint almost non-existent. The place had gone unrepaired for years, the heavy wooden door would surely fall off its hinges if you dared to try and open it.

'There is scope for improvement of course and lots of room for more...' he came up behind her, placed his arms round her and stroked the bump.

She turned to look at her husband, her lifelong friend and soulmate, eyes wet with tears.

'Lucy. NO! No don't...I'm sorry.' He took her hand and turned to lead her back to the van. He didn't expect the resistance and when he turned back and saw the tears that were streaming now. He struggled to hide his disappointment.

'Dan.' Lucy whispered, 'it's perfect.'

Four weeks later the van trundled up the lane again, this time without Lucy, a bed strapped on the roof and a couple of chairs in the back. The old oak table that had been left in the kitchen had been scrubbed and sanded by Dan, and he, Reg and some friends from their old village had put up a fence and repaired the smaller of the barns, later he would reclaim the larger, more derelict one, but for now that would be home to the one hundred sheep which were due to arrive in a couple days. He couldn't help thinking that the prospect of the sheep scared him much less than the arrival of the child due any day now.

'DAN!' He turned to see a man on a bike coming through the gateway. It looked like… 'DAN NOW!' It *was* Nathan. Their old post man, did he really come all this way too? 'Dan, I'm so sorry, we had a phone call, from the hospital. It's Lucy, Dan. She's having the baby. NOW!' He gasped for some breath, it was a long, hilly trip.

'But she only went for a check-up!' He tore across to the van, leaving several men speechless and uncertain in the garden.

'I am so *sorry*,' Lucy sobbed over and over again.

Dan held on tight to her, wiped her tears and his own and replied slowly and carefully to his distraught wife. 'It. Is. Not. Your. Fault.'

'But it is!' She cried again and turned on her side pulling the covers over her head.

Dan gently pulled them away and stroked her hair. 'NO. It isn't. Stillbirths and baby complications, they run in your family, that can't be helped. I love you Lucy Collier,' he cradled her face as he wiped her eyes with his thumbs, 'with or without children. Do I make myself clear?' He kissed the top of her head. A lump in his throat as he thought of the son he, they, had wanted so badly. Life was cruel sometimes but he would *never* let Lucy think it was her fault. He was lucky to have found her and, for that, he would be eternally grateful.

The first time Dan had laid eyes on Lucy he had been just 7 years old and new to the school, along with his brother Phillip. He knew he was in love with her there and then, her tiny face and hands, the tresses of gold. He was entranced. They had built a close friendship but, as they got older, he couldn't pluck up the courage to ask her out properly. He consoled himself with the fact that no-one else could either. They had moved here to live with their grandparents, their own parents having died in a fall. That was all they told him and for a long while he was terrified that falling over would kill you! His grandparents had patiently explained one day, when they had found him hysterical after tripping on the door step, that no, his mummy and daddy had fallen a *long* way. They had been walking along a cliff edge and the path was wet, his daddy had reached out to stop his mummy falling and they had both gone over the edge. They hadn't wanted to tell him till he was older as they felt he was too young to need the details.

One afternoon he was out cycling and saw Lucy rushing out of the woods at the end of the village and wanted to show off his new bike. It was actually old but his grandfather, in his "magic shed", had rebuilt and painted it, so it looked like new. When he reached Lucy, she had seemed upset and although he had chatted to her for ages, she never did tell him what was wrong but when she avoided the gaze of a boy coming down the road, he had a good idea. That first hour he spent with her had made him certain that she was "the one" that his grandad was always banging on about. "Your grandma? I just knew she was the one for me the minute I saw her." he was frequently heard to say. Now, looking at the blonde waves and bright blue eyes in front of him, he knew, deep inside, he knew now exactly what he meant. He didn't even mind when she called him "Rusty, 'cos of your chestnut hair". Their first kiss had been at the village fete, he had just beaten all records with the coconuts and gave Lucy the teddy bear that he won, she had giggled and cuddled it, then pecked his cheek, quite shyly. He was *so* hooked. He spent the next week working up to the real thing. Now *that* had been the high point of his life so far. Until, in what seemed an unseasonably warm November, or maybe it was just the heat of the moment, when the bonfire party was going strong on the village green they had slipped away and, not hearing the oohs and aahs of the crowds watching the fireworks, she had become really his. When she had said yes to his request some weeks after he felt his happiness was complete. He looked down at the now sleeping form. So, it wasn't the end of the world if they didn't have children. He had the cake, he didn't need the icing. Did he? He sighed deeply as he left the hospital. Next time he told himself. Next time it *will* be fine.

Lucy threw herself into the farm when she returned and soon there were pretty curtains at the windows, the frames painted a bright shade of yellow with a matching, now usable, thanks to Dan and Phil's handiwork learnt from long hours with their grandad, front door with a brass knocker and handle which she shined weekly. Dan had made a stable door on the side entrance into the kitchen so Lucy could look out towards the barns and out the window to the fields, the angle of the house also allowed her a view of the lane too, so she felt as if she was in a huge open space and connected to everything and everyone. The tiled kitchen floor, which had been scrubbed to within an inch of its life, by Lucy on her hands and knees, had a woven rug, which she had made in the evenings from old scraps of material, in front of the Aga. A basket next to it ready for the puppy they were expecting. They had been rounding up the sheep with Reg's dog but she was getting old now, "like me" he'd joked, so Dan was getting a helper of his own while she could still help with its training. Outside, Lucy had started on her own little bit of a kitchen garden, a rickety fence round it for the moment as the wall wasn't repaired fully, there was *still* no gate, and she didn't want escaping sheep, of which there were many, eating her new shoots. It also helped to keep in the chickens she was using to dig over and manure the ground for her. So much easier to put ten of them on the patch for a few days, they scratched and pooed for a while and then she could just rake it over and it was ready for planting. Reg was full of useful tips. Chicken manure made great fertilizer she had been assured, if a bit stinky. Lucy stopped scrubbing the table and stood up, her back ached and…NO! so did her belly. Come to think of it, when *was* her last monthly pain, the cleaning, the repairing, the making things…the last few months had been a bit of blur really. Then she rushed to the sink and promptly threw up…over all Dan's overalls that were soaking there. She rubbed her back then gently placed a hand on her tummy, sending up a silent prayer for the new baby she was now sure was forming inside her. Unexpectedly, she felt that this time…this time things were going to be alright.

And this time …they had been.

How had life changed so quickly and dramatically! Neither Dan nor Lucy could not believe how exhausting it was having twins. Well, actually it was really only one of them. Jessica was a dream. She slept, she woke, she fed, she slept. Amelia? She fed, she threw up, she screamed, she cried, she fed, she threw up. She slept, then when Jess was asleep, she woke and she screamed. She was a *nightmare*. But they loved her, cared for her, laughed as much as they could and eventually both the girls settled down. Then came the temper tantrums. Amy didn't get her own way? AAAHHH. Didn't like her tea? AAAHHH. Didn't want to wear this that or the other?

AAAHHH. Usually followed by tearing the said item off and throwing it on the floor. Lucy loved both her girls equally. But Amy made it hard. REALLY hard! As they became toddlers Jess would sit still playing with a doll, all dressed up and ready to go out in her pretty frocks with her silky blonde hair in a bow. So would Amy. For five minutes. Then they would find her outside, rolling in the dust, trying to be like the chickens! She would end up in her old clothes to go out as there was nothing else available. They looked like the princess and the pauper every time they went anywhere. When Dan was sowing the fields for the winter sheep feed he would find Amy in a pair of his old overalls, rolled up sleeves and legs, old boots and his favourite hat, standing in the middle of the field, with a big toothy grin, being a "scare*cow*."

Chapter Three

'Bye girls, you will be fine.' Lucy tidied their collars and pulled Amy's hair a little bit tighter, it was always *so* uncontrollable. 'Yes, Jessica, your dad will remember to feed the lambs.' The twins were dressed in their blue and yellow school uniforms, holding bags bigger than they were, ready to come home full, of what she hadn't a clue, but they were part of the requirements. She wiped the tears from her daughter's eyes as the bus driver hmphed, his patience had run out. Honestly, why drive the school bus if you don't like kids? Lucy quickly hugged both girls, Jessica's blonde straight hair and Amelia's uncontrollable ginger curls both smelt of strawberries as she kissed the top of their heads. She teased them that their dad drunk so much Amy came out rusty! After watching them go she turned to pick up the dolls and toys the girls had left on the table. Smiling she lifted the toy tractor, Amy's favourite. That girl was *such* a tomboy. Dan had kind of got his son, after all! Anything she could be involved with she had her nose in. Both girls helped round the farm but Amy positively revelled in it. Mud didn't faze her nor the birth of the lambs, she was *always* dirty and in the little overalls Dan had bought them both with "Dad's little helper" stitched across the front. Jessica's pair were worn only on occasion and never involved soaking before washing, unlike Dan and Amy's. When she was two she had picked up a spanner and hit the tractor with it, the noise made Dan jump but before he could say anything she had said, quite clearly, "helping Dad". Jessica on the other hand loved to help in the kitchen. The girls had matching aprons for this and both were equally messy in that challenge. Jess was a good cook and, surprisingly, so was Amy, but she was always distracted and itching to go back to the barns. Barney had now been coached into giving Amy his paw and rolling over, not ideal training for a sheep dog! and he would take commands from her as easily as he would Dan. This had led to some interesting viewing as the sheep were driven backwards and forwards through the field. They must end up so confused, she thought as they were chased to the left for the fifth time in as many minutes. Next, she would see Amy running back towards the house and she knew Dan had found an "urgent" message for her. It usually involved a cup of tea. Good idea that. She filled the kettle and lit the gas. Not sure what to do first. She needed to kill some time while she waited for a lift. However, when she climbed in the rusty white van, she was reminded why she usually walked. Wet, stale and chemically. It stank!

'MONA! I am so pleased for you.' Lucy hugged her sister, pretending not to notice her wrinkling her nose. She had decided to visit to take her mind off the twins, and the news was fantastic, she was expecting another baby! It was now five months and everything was fine, she had been assured.

'We are hoping for a girl this time, just to even things up, like. And at least this one won't be sharing a birthday with yours.' Mona had gone into labour the day before the twins first birthday and had her son just seconds after midnight, so much so there was a lot of watch synchronising, but she had still insisted on coming home in time for the family party. She passed Lucy a cup of tea and was shaking so much it spilled all over the white lace cloth.

'I'll do it.' Lucy jumped to her feet and let Mona sit down. 'I've been playing mother longer than you.'

'Only by a year!' She smiled good naturedly and watched her son, now four, playing farms on the floor. 'He adores your place you know. Every time we visit you he talks of nothing but "fluffy sheeps" and "pooey chickens", for days.'

'Dan loves it when you come over you know, he would have really loved a boy.' Lucy and Dan had long since given up any thoughts of that idea, when Mona and Phil had had a boy Dan took to the role of uncle immediately and now they were contented with their two girls, in fact with Amy being so attached to Dan, she was almost like a little mini-me, but with her beautiful long red curls Lucy did manage to ensure her younger daughter maintained at least an image of femininity.

Later that afternoon Lucy watched for the bus and anxiously wrung her hands and fiddled with her apron strings as two very excited little girls got off and ran up the path.

'Mummy we...ow.' Jess pushed her sister out of the way and protested.

'I want to tell her! Mummy they split us up and Amy had to sit next to a *boy*!'

'Well, that's not so bad is it?' She rubbed the red curls and laughed, 'he could be your first boyfriend.' She teased with a smile. 'What's his name?' She was very surprised when Amy threw down her bag and stomped off towards the door. 'Mike, and I *hate* boys!' She stamped her foot.

'Now then, go and change.' Lucy looked at the fiery little bundle in front of her, redheads she thought, with a sigh. She looked at Jessie and added, 'you too, those lambs don't feed themselves, do they? Your dad needs a hand.' She smiled and was amazed as Jess and Amy went thundering up and down the stairs, changed, and out the door at lightning speed. Lucy felt suddenly tired, then she felt a familiar pain she sat down, placing a hand on the slight swelling of her belly. Aww, not again!

'Mummy, fresh from the cows' tits!' They chorused as they carried a bucket in between them.

'TEATS! Girls. They are teats. T.E.A.T.S.' She reprimanded. Trying very hard not to laugh.

'That's not what Daddy calls them!' They giggled and ran back to the barn. Laughing and pushing each other and doing high fives. They learnt that at school then.

School should be a time for children to start to mingle and mix and grow friendships that could last a lifetime. This was not so for Amy.

'It wasn't my fault!' the foot went down and Lucy looked first at the teacher then back to her youngest daughter. 'He called me a…' she stopped and went over to whisper in Lucy's ear. Lucy quickly stifled the laugh that threatened and pulled a suitable straight face.

'Did he now? Well, that isn't very nice is it? But I don't think it needed you to pour water all over his painting. Do you?'

'YES!'

'Amy?'

'Nooo.' She looked under her eyelids at her mother and held her hands behind her back unable to keep still.

'Apologise then.'

'But!' Her eyes widened as she looked towards the boy on the other chair.

'Now please.'

'Sorry.' She looked at the floor. Then, to her Mummy, 'Don't tell Daddy?'

'He called her a carrot top so she threw water over his picture? Oh well, don't suppose we have to worry about her being bullied then. Serious retaliation!'

'It isn't really funny is it? *She* will get the bully reputation if she carries on like that.' Lucy handed Dan a mug of tea on his way out. She *was* getting a little worried about her but then, she supposed, she would grow out of it.

'You want *what* for your birthday?' Lucy and Dan looked at their daughter then at each other. 'I don't see why not?' Dan looked at Lucy. 'But you must have complete responsibility for it. Okay?' He said sternly.

Amy did an air punch. 'Yes! I will Dad, I will, I want to train it, to do tricks and stuff?' She was really getting excited now.

'A pet chicken, she could just have one anyway?' Dan queried over a cup of tea.

'She's eight. If it's what she wants it's fine. Just make sure you don't get the wrong one in for the Sunday lunch!' Lucy, making toad in the hole, waved a limp sausage at him and laughed.

'With a weapon like that in your hands I wouldn't dare get anything wrong!' The phone rang and he left Lucy to answer it. He didn't get very far.

'I need you to take me to the school. It's Amy. There's been another fight.' They sighed in unison.

The birthday party for the twins tenth, and their cousins ninth, was a large event, due to some unusually warm weather, but Amy sat alone on the tree swing with Barney at her side dribble all over her flowery dress.

'There you are, c'mon your friends are waiting to cut the cake.' Her mums hand reached out for her, but she flinched away.

'They're not *my* friends! They are Jess's and yours.' She kicked the ground with her glittery shoes.

'Don't ruin those!' then, softer, she added, 'come on, you like cake,' Barney pricked up his ears. 'Yes, and so do you, but you can only have a tiny piece.' To Amy she added 'It's chocolate…'

Amy let out a huge sigh. Jess had many friends. Girlfriends. She had included Amy many, many times in her playdates but Amy just wouldn't play with dolls, or shops or talk about clothes and hair and eventually she would just wander off and find one of the animals. And now there was no one for her to ask to the party. The boys wouldn't even entertain the idea. "A party! They're for girls. Not likely!". They had said in unison when she had suggested they could come. She tugged the ribbon out of her hair threw it on the floor and ran off towards the barn.

'*And,* I am never wearing a dress again. EVER.' She shouted behind her. The dog, very torn between cake and his favourite person, chose dutifully to run after Amy, but she ran up the ladder and sulked in the hay bales so he settled down to wait for her, his head on his paws. Experience told him she could be a while.

'Why did you do that!?' Jess cried picking up the broken doll.

Amy shrugged. 'Just wanted to see how it was made.'

'But you broke it!' She cried out as their dad came in.

'Now I am sure she didn't mean to, did you Amy,' he stared at the girl at the top of the stairs. 'Did you, Amy,'

'S'pose not.'

'Give it here. I am sure I can fix it.' He held out his hand. He was getting used to fixing things at the moment. Amy seemed to be having some sort of destructive phase. Everything she touched she wanted to take apart! Last week the wheel was missing off of the wheel barrow and the week before he had walked in the lounge and found the back of the TV on the floor, Amy behind it about to stick her fingers inside. It was still plugged in. And switched on! He had decided to give in and buy her a Meccano set and hoped that would keep her occupied. In the mean time she was "helping" him to take machinery apart in the barn so it could be oiled and put back together. If she could manage without losing bits it would be a miracle.

Amy looked at her sister and mumbled 'I'm sorry.' And, really, she was. She wouldn't hurt her sister, she just wanted to see to see if there were any parts inside the doll. Like people had, and animals. Her dad's face, when he found her poking about in the dead ewe she found in the field! She was just fascinated by, "all that being able to fit inside there!" The only time he had seen her upset was over the live-stock was when she had first nursed a lamb, for three days, and it hadn't made it. She thought it was her fault as the others had been fine. He had taken days to convince her to do another one. That time it was okay. Ironic really, as they had to go for slaughter anyway. But he was bringing them up to understand where food came from and that felt…right.

'It's alright, Dad will fix it. Just stop being so…so weird.' Jess left.

Thirteen Dan sighed, thirteen. This is just the start! Later that week Amy entered the barn holding a gun. 'Dad, what are you doing with this?'

He was quick to respond. Gently taking it off of her. He had thought they were all in town and hadn't put it away yet. 'I had to shoot some…erm, anyway, what are you doing back so soon?'

'Oh, I didn't want to go so I said I had a headache.' She looked at the gun again. 'Could you teach me, Dad?'

'But you don't like to harm the wildlife?' He replied, somewhat surprised.

'Oh. No, I only want to shoot targets, like tins and things.'

After teaching her the safety aspects Dan set up a little shooting range for her using tins and old, he hoped, plates, setting them all out at different distances. He could not believe what an impressive shot she was. If he hadn't had to spend hours teaching her the right way to hold the gun, he'd have thought she had been learning behind his back. When she got the hang of it there was no stopping her. Her aim was incredible! As with most things though she soon grew bored of it.

Chapter Four

'C'mon, Ginge!' Mike hit Amy on the shoulder, none too gently, as he ran past, pushing her off the wall as she sat outside the school gates. 'We're going down the sweet shop.'

The usual lunchtime spot she thought, though for sweets read fags. She grabbed her bag and followed Mike, watching as he gave Tony and Dave a joint head-slap when he caught them up, then they all headed down the road towards the village square. She hoped they would keep the space under the tree so she didn't get burnt. Or worse, freckly!

She tried smoking and, even when it had made her gag, she persevered as she hadn't wanted to look like a girl, in front of the boys but it wasn't for her. Amy knew her mother didn't like her spending so much time with the boys, especially after the hair incident.

Some girls had held her down "want to be like the boys? Then you'd better look like one." Bloody Tina Saunders and her crew, they had almost scalped her! Could she help it if she preferred being with them, the smell, the excitement, even the pool matches. The football? Not so much, but then who liked everything? They called her Mike's little shadow but she wasn't – not really – she liked being with all of them, even when they made fun of her she took it in her stride. It was part of belonging, wasn't it? They also called her Mike's "girlfriend in waiting" but she wasn't. No, definitely not. Then he would give her that look, the secret one that they shared, that made her feel he understood, that he knew how she felt, deep down. Amy shivered and looked down at her trousers knowing she would be in trouble for the ripped knees, again, her mum having given up ages ago on making her wear skirts. "Why can't you be more like Jessica?" Her mum was so fond of saying. But she didn't blame her sister, they adored each other. Most of the time.

'Yuch, must you do that?' Jess scolded Amy as she blew smoke in her face. 'Mum will *kill* you if she finds out.'
'Yeah. But she won't, will she?'
'She will if you set fire to the hay bales again!' They both giggled at the shared memory. Jess had startled her when she had been having a sneaky cigarette round behind the barn and she had dropped the lit ciggie onto the haybale, the girls grabbed a bucket each as, fortunately, there was a water trough nearby.
'Trust you to bring that up again. Hey wait for us!' The girls hurried to catch up.
'Hurry up twiglets you'll be late.' Mike called back.

That evening, in a rare moment of peace between Amy and her mum, Lucy asked 'So, Amy, what would you like for your birthday?' Amy knew *exactly* what she wanted but she wasn't going to tell her mum *that*! 'I can't believe my girls are going to be 16.' Lucy went on. Amy waited for the, "it doesn't seem like 5 minutes" speech that, thankfully, didn't arrive due to Jessica barging through the door with Simon in tow. Honestly, he looked like a bloody puppy, she almost expected to see him dribble! Amy got up to leave as she wasn't in the mood for her mother's other pet saying right now, "Isn't it time *you* got a proper boyfriend?" She got it anyway.

They knew she hung around with Mike but he was going places, no village life for him. Oh no. He wanted Uni, a law degree and, maybe, a professorship to finish it off. No, Amy needed to find a nice village lad not hanker after someone expecting "the high life". Her parent's words usually followed by, "your dad and I met at school, we were childhood sweethearts," then came the secret smile, "now look at us, happy as" then dad would finish "a squirrel in an oak tree." Yuch! but the thought of her dad made her smile and, that being a good excuse, she left, 'going to help Dad.'

As she wandered out of the door Barney, the collie, followed and licked her hand, his usual sign that he knew she was a little low. She scuffed at the dust as she crossed the yard to the ancient brick barn. She loved her sister and Mum really, she did, but she always felt so out of it, they were so...so... *girly*. Amy felt far happier in trainers and riding her bike. Now that would be a good present, her own motorbike! No chance! Maybe a scooter? Just something to get her further away than the two little isolated villages.

'Dad, Dad are you in there.' Funny she thought, then heard a scuffling behind her in the smaller barn opposite and her father appeared round the door, wiping his hands on a rag. Amy briefly wondered if it was a nervous thing

– he was always doing it – but she guessed not. Nothing stressed her dad...EVER! Even her mum rarely raised a voice for more than one sentence, the thought struck her that they were actually a nice, normal family in every way, so, what was wrong with her then? According to Lucy and Simon's mum, Kate, it was "hormones". She had overheard her mum and her talking over *another* glass of wine and Kate, who only had boys, was spouting forth about hormones. What the hell did she know. She was *old* though, so Amy did at least consider the idea that she could be right after all. 'Hi Dad, need a hand?'

'Actually, I do, I'm going to the shops and I could use some company.' His eyes twinkled at her the same as always but she thought he looked a bit tired, he'd also been sitting down more too, she realised. Amy smiled and knew that was Dad's way of keeping them busy. If nothing needed doing that they could help with he always, "needed company". She hugged him as they walked to the old, dirty van.

'I'll wash this if you like, when we get back?'

'Ok, precious.' He grinned, both knowing full well she wouldn't.

'A pack of the green twine, and I need some new shears please, the smaller ones. Thanks.' While her dad was served Amy, bored now, wandered around the shop floor then brightened at the sight out the window. She kissed her dad and rushed out the door, after promising she'd be back for tea. Simon and his parents were coming over...deep joy!

'Mike, Mike...wait.' Did he just *roll* his eyes?

'Hi Amy, what you doing?'

'Wondered if you fancy an ice-cream?' She knew he never said no to that one. Bingo.

'Oh, yeah, great thanks.' He relaxed a bit.

She hadn't meant it as her treat but she couldn't back out now. They found a quiet corner to sit on the green and eat them. She always had rum and raisin in the childish belief that she was drinking alcohol! Mike never had the same one twice and, after lots of dithering, with Amy hopping from foot to foot, all the time wondering how someone who was so serious could be so wavering, finally he chose...vanilla, plain old vanilla! Honestly, boys. If *I* was a boy, I would be far more decisive, she decided!

'So, next week then? Sweet sixteen and never been kissed,' he joked with her...at least she *thought* he was joking. He wasn't. He leant his head towards her and...NO!

She dropped the now tilting ice-cream down her front and shot to her feet. 'Oh…!' Amy rushed off down the road just in time to catch her dad coming up the lane and the look she threw him, as she got in, had the desired effect.

'Alright love.' Which she took as a statement, not a question.

That evening Amy opened the door to Simon's parents, all smiles now, the earlier, "Mike" incident forgotten. For the moment. 'Mum and Dad are out the back and the barbie's on the go, so we can expect the fire brigade any time soon.' Laughter followed and her dad's voice behind added, 'Don't be so cheeky young lady, Lucy is out the back Kate,' he greeted her with the usual kiss and went to get Barry a beer.

She heard their voices fade as she went up to get her jacket. Through the open window her mum and Kate's conversation flowed in.

'Of course, Simon is very keen on Jess, and you know we love her to bits, young love is so *sweet* isn't it?'

Oh god, Kate was as bad as her mother.

'Yes, who knows we could be making wedding plans this time next year!' They sounded so excited. Amy cringed as she heard the happiness within her mother's voice. She hurried back down to join the others. Unknown to her and Jessica the family had also been invited as a surprise early birthday party for them. Aunt Mona, not known for her culinary skills, had even made them a cake. She and Jess had a bet on exactly how hard it would be and whether the ducks would sink if fed it! It was a wonder her children survived on her cooking.

The sisters and their cousin were called to blow out the candles and, as she joined Jess by the table they were serenaded, their mum cried that her girls, "were all grown up now", to anyone still listening. The party, as always, went on until very late, or early depending on your viewpoint, and the girls drifted off to sleep to the clinking of glass downstairs. Amy wondered how different life would be now she was an adult, then realised, in a sleepy haze, that she wasn't, not yet, *that* would have to wait till she was 18.

On Monday's bus Amy felt a sharp tug to her hair and Mike appeared in front of her.

'Hey, Ames, listen I'm having a bit of a party Friday night after we break up – you know a leaving school at last thing. You up for it? He stared into her eyes. It had been 3 weeks since the 'incident' and nothing had been said, or changed, she opened her mouth to reply but Mike was already walking off up the aisle. 'Great, knew you would, see you 'bout 7.'

She sighed, five whole days left at school, five more slow, painful days...she couldn't wait to leave.

Friday morning, before school, their mum gave them a special breakfast, held them in a group hug and said, 'now you're all grown up but you will always be my little girls and I will do *anything* for you. Anything to help or protect you. That's what a mother is for, it's our natural instinct.' She kissed them both once more and pushed them outside to wait for the bus for the last time.

Jess tugged her at sister's sleeve as they sat on the tatty blue bus. 'Amy, what do you think we'll get tomorrow from Mum and Dad?'

'Dunno,' Amy shrugged, then added, 'Jess, I was going to go into to town tomorrow, to try and find a job?'

'What! On our birthday? NO WAY.' Amy's hurt must've shown on her face so Jess relented, 'I'll come on Monday, if you like?'

'Yeah, whatever.' Amy turned away and looked out the window. 'Hey, Mr Simm's broken down again,' Amy nudged her sister as she pointed to the tractor in the middle of the field and the figure marching down the hill.

'Should've asked Dad, Dad can fix *anything!'* Jess said. Amy truly wished that were so.

Everyone was in happy mode at school, although the usual bitchiness kicked in when they saw Amy was still in school uniform. She'd cheeked her parents and this was her punishment, such as it was, trainers and trousers weren't all that different to trainers and jeans really, and she always wore plain shirts or tee's anyway. Today no one had any work to do, it was simply a case of attend and be counted so all around she could hear talk of shopping trips in town straight after registration. By lunch time most of the year were missing, only to turn up later for the bus, a few the worse for wear as some idiot had served them a load of alcohol. The driver exploded when one of the boys threw up at the back of the coach and he was booed and jeered all the way home. Mike, surprisingly, was on the bus tonight and he breathed fume filled air onto Amy and Jess as he slurred, 'she yoose la'er.' And flicked his hand in the air leaving a finger pointing at Amy and went to join the boys further back where a lot of noisy laughter ensued. Amy blushed.

'What's that about?' Jess asked her sister.

'He's just drunk,' she said, then added 'you know I'm sleeping over at Elaine's tonight, you were invited too but,' she sang,' you're going out with Simon,' then finished it with, 'and your in-laws.' Amy nearly choked on her laughter. Jess punched her arm.

The pride on their dad's face as the girls came down for a lift to their respective evenings was obvious.
'Wow! Where are my little girls and who are you?' Jess had curled her hair and swept it up to one side. She was wearing a pale blue satin dress pinched at the waist with no sleeves and pretty low-heeled sandals, she looked as if she was ready for a photo shoot. Secretly, Amy thought she looked like a sacrificial offering but kept quiet. Everyone knew that Simon was going to, have the talk, that evening about their future, with only the *slightest* push from *both* sets of parents.
Amy was wearing the usual jeans and tee with the favoured trainers still hugging her feet.
'Amy, where *is* Elaine's house?' Their dad looked around as he came into the village.
'Oh, I'll just get out with Jess, it's only up the road.' Amy saw Jess's mouth open but she didn't manage more than a squeak when Amy kicked her ankle as she mouthed, 'shut up.'
They hugged each other as the tatty van drove away and Amy watched her sister walk up to Simon's front door, and the future that lay beyond it, Jess turned to her and blew a kiss before walking in the front door. Amy hitched up her rucksack and turned to walk, the opposite direction from Elaine's, towards the big detached houses at the other end of the small village. Big fish, small pond was her parent's favourite saying about the area. The one

she was heading for was partly hidden by a high hedge and set back on the plot leaving room for three large and one small car. To the left a double garage and behind this, in a corner of the park-sized garden, was a swimming pool. Amy went around the side of the house and let herself in through the unlocked gate, surprised there was no bouncy, dribbling dog to greet her. She could see Mike laying on the pool sofa.

'Where's Skipper?' she asked.

As he opened just the one eye, he put his hand to his head, 'christ, my eyes, my head.' He groaned.

Amy decided he needed coffee and went into the smart, modern kitchen. As she entered she couldn't hear anyone about, normally by now Anna, Mike's older sister, would have at least ignored her! She hadn't seen the big SUV out front either. Finding the milk in the silver American style fridge she pulled out a lemonade for herself and pressed the switch for the ice dispenser, she *loved* that bit.

She left the house and went back outside to find Mike. He was now upright, however, there was a pile of green vomit at his feet. What the hell had he drunk? He must have seen the disgust on her face.

'I have no idea, the lads were here till about five and we were drinking anything and everything. God, I need a shower. OW! that's hot.' He put down the coffee and headed off to the pool showers, which, Amy knew, also contained spare clothes in case, as was a frequent occurrence, someone *accidentally* fell in fully clothed.

She busied herself with the hose to clear away the bright puddle. As she worked, she took in her surroundings. This was clearly a fabulous lifestyle; one she'd never afford on the wages she would soon be taking home. What did his parents do? She knew it was something legal but that sort of thing was beyond her and she hadn't been that interested when Mike had tried to explain it.

'Anyone in there?' There was a sharp pull on her pony-tail and she turned to face him, now armed with a drink that smelled like whisky. Ugh.

'How can you? After that!' Her arm swung towards the wet spot on the floor.

'Easy, oh you *did* clean.' He sounded as though he'd expected it and she wondered if sometimes she wasn't just a little too eager to please. She sipped her drink then pulled a face. 'Tastes weird.'

'I expect you're not used to that make…it's 'spensive.' He was slurring again. Amy wasn't sure she liked *this* Mike.

'Where's your family?'

'They're away taking Anna to see schools.' Of *course* they were. Anna and Amy had a mutual dislike of each other – Amy thought Anna stuck up - and in return Anna didn't think Amy was good enough to hang out with her little brother. Their parents, on the other hand, were easy going, or just not interested in what their son was up to, Anna though was cosseted and enrolled in every club in the area that would enable her to make a "good match". Her own parent's ideas for Jess and Simon made her think that perhaps they weren't so different after all.

'Hey, Ginge, come and play Supermario, I feel like a winner.' Amy agreed. In that state, she'd seen his shaky hands, she couldn't lose.

An hour later, with Amy leading four games to three, Mike threw the controller at the screen on the wall just as the door pushed open and three boys arrived.

'What! A *girl*?' A voice that Amy didn't recognise at first sounded really put out. Then realised it was Stuart, Tony Hodder's older brother.

'Nah. It's just Ames, she's no girl.' She wasn't quite sure how to take that one!

'Still maybe a girl's a good idea, later?' Amy stayed quiet as there followed some crude moves and suggestions.

'Isn't there a girly sleep over at Elaine's place?' Tony asked.

'Yeah, but there's a mum in residence.' Added Dave, who lived next to her.

'Fantasy football Mike?'

'Course, but get the drinks and stuff first.'

Amy bloody hated fantasy football, so she kept score and fetched more drinks and snacks. Just to be there was enough to keep her happy. For now. She lost count of how many drinks they'd all had but there were two whisky bottles in the bin, and as the boys were losing in the football rounds, they staggered through to the pool table, where Amy could come into her own.

She was really good at pool and soon thrashed three of them. As she racked up for a game with Mike, she suddenly felt the boy's eyes on her from around the room. One of them commented on the fact that, for a tomboy, Amy had a *very* nice arse. She straightened up, to see the boy at the end of the table...he was staring straight down her top and, embarrassed, she tugged at it and turned away...only to be pressed back against the table by one of the others, who was now right behind her.

'Nice tits too, tiny, but nice.' He leered.

Amy sensed a change in the atmosphere and tried to joke it off. 'Yeah, but yours are bigger.'

The boy didn't move. Then in one quick, seemingly practised, move he reached out and ripped the front of her top down.

'Mike, please...Mike?' Her eyes searched frantically for him. But, when she saw his face, she realised...no one would help her...no one would save her...no one would protect her...and...no one would hear her scream.

Chapter Five

'Amy...Amy? *Please* Amy.' Her mum knocked on the door again, her voice pleading now,

'GO AWAY! You don't understand. You don't understand *me*!'

Lucy tried again, despite knowing it to be perfectly true. She *really* didn't understand her daughter, but she *was* her daughter and she wanted to help her. 'Amy if you still aren't well you really need the doctor. Darling it's been over a *week* now! Please talk to me.'

Amy didn't care if it had been a month; she wasn't in a hurry to ever go outside again! She wasn't sure if her mum did believe she was ill or if she thought she was upset over Mike leaving, either way she wasn't budging! And she certainly didn't want a doctor. She had gone over and over that night every minute of every day for the last week, she had even missed her birthday and that had caused a right fuss, the last thing she wanted, but she couldn't tell them, not even Jess and she told her *everything*. Well, almost. This was different though, no-one must *ever* know about this. And Mike? How could she have been so *wrong* about Mike? She thought he knew, thought he *understood*. She couldn't remember it all. It was a blur after the first two. She knew it was all four of them but she had just switched off. It still felt surreal, she thought of their faces as she left, nothing registered on them...nothing at all…No compassion, no guilt or remorse...nothing. They sat, sipping their beers and shouting at the screen as she crept out through the patio doors and into the dark.

Jess had told her, told her back actually, that Mike had left the village and was going to stay with family elsewhere *and* go to a different sixth-form as his parents came home to a trashed house after a weekend away, so she knew she wouldn't have to face him, but the others? Amy pulled the covers back over her head.

Even when her dad had been up to see her and kissed her head she didn't move, just flinched away from him. She felt the hurt from him but couldn't even feel guilty. Amy knew she would have to surface soon and perhaps it would be better sooner than later. She made up her mind and shuffled into the bathroom, showered, went downstairs, took a deep breath and pushed open the door.

'How about a piece of my cake Mum?' She tried hard not to flinch as her mum hugged tighter than ever.

She could not believe it! They *had* got her a scooter, granted not a new one, but Dads fiddling in the small barn now made sense, he could fix anything after all. She suppressed the little voice trying to shout, "no, he can't" and hugged them both. 'But what about Jess?' she asked, 'what did she get?'

'Ah, now she wanted a watch so that's what she got.'

'And this,' Jess joined them and held out her left hand, a tiny little diamond chip sparkled on it, 'glad you're feeling better sis.' She hugged Amy.

Amy nearly said, 'are you sure' but her mum pre-empted her.

'Of course, they have to wait a year first before they are allowed to start planning it.' She saw her daughter frowning and added, 'but I think we all know it will be fine.' looking at her husband he nodded his agreement.

'Best start saving luv.'

'Of course, you just *have* to be my bridesmaid!'

'I wish I'd stayed in bed! Kidding. Just promise me one thing…NO pink taffeta!' Amy laughed for the first time in weeks.

'Can't promise.' Jess grinned. 'Kidding!'

A few days later Amy came in and couldn't move for reams of cream silk. She should have known that her mother would start the wedding dress as soon as she could stating, "she didn't have a lot of spare time and it would take her a lot of fittings before it was finished". Yeah right. Wanted to ensure it went ahead more like.

'Mum, have you finished my jeans yet?' Amy asked, then quickly answered for her, 'no. I haven't had time.'

'Yes, I have! They're over there.' Right, point scored to Mum.

Upstairs, Amy put on the new jeans as she was going into town, time to find a job. She still hadn't been into the village...couldn't, but she had been sitting round the farmhouse *way* too much the lately. Much more than she realised. She struggled to pull up the zip.

'Don't forget I need *you* for a fitting later. Good luck.' Lucy called.

At least she was going to be wearing dark blue even if it *was* bloody satin! Amy grimaced.

'Amy, you have to stop eating your way through that shop you work at.' Lucy sighed as she went to unpick the bridesmaid dress all over again. 'I can't keep doing this, the material just won't take all this fiddling.'

Amy sat and picked at the remains of the cake on the table.

'AMY! Did you hear a word I said?' Lucy took the cake away. 'Honestly, sometimes you seem like you're just not here anymore. This is your sister's big day we're sorting out you know?'

Know! Know? There was no escaping the fucking thing! She snatched up her bag and stomped up the stairs and slammed the bedroom door.

Sitting on her bed she pulled out the small, plastic strip...and focused, still disbelieving, at the blue line in the little window.

Chapter Six

Amy finally went back downstairs. She had put the plastic test in the bathroom bin and then, realising her error she shot back in, put it in her pocket, and went out to the incinerator. Her mother didn't notice as she was still waist high in taffeta and satin. She did notice enough though to call after her to fetch some dog food. That put the escape by bike out of the equation.

Over in the barn she soon found the food packs and as she climbed up to get them, she fell off the ladder. That was when the idea hit her. If she fell hard enough, maybe, just maybe? She climbed up to the hayloft. Walked to the edge. Closed her eyes. And…
'Amy, Amy are you in here?'
She looked down and realised with horror, had she jumped, she would have landed on her dad. Some straw had slipped off, causing him to look up, straight at her.
'There you are.' He looked, as always, pleased to see her. Then he frowned. 'Aren't you a little old for that game now?' He knew the girls had always loved jumping into the deep hay when they were little. 'And there's not much there either.' He kicked at it, it only came to the top of his battered, old black wellies. 'Your mum needs a hand, folding the dress stuff.' He held up his hands, 'I'm not allowed near it with these. I snag, apparently.' He shrugged his shoulders. 'Dare say she's right, your mother usually is.' They shared a

conspiratorial smile and Amy tucked the idea away and went down to join her dad.

CRACK.

'AAHH!'

One of the rungs broke and Amy fell backwards.

'Easy love! You'll have an accident.' Her dad broke her fall and hugged her tight. 'That was close. OK? Good, go in then. I'll fix this in no time.'

Dad all over, Amy thought, fixes everything. Not this time the little voice inside said, refusing to be silent. She bent to pick up the dog food and felt the zip pop on her jeans.

'Wow, someone ate all the pies! *that* is one of the things your mother fixes.'

Amy stropped off to fold the fragile material.

'Not *again*! Go and change them then, no, help me first. I'll fix them later, I except you want them back for work tomorrow?'

Amy, grateful that her mother wasn't asking any questions, turned away as her eyes welled. 'No, I'm…it's okay, I'll find something else.' She had just come *so* close to telling her. The look of surprise on her mother's face caused her to return to normal teenage operating mode, 'yeah, well, whenever, whatever.'

'Really Amy, I hope you aren't that rude to the customers or you won't keep that job five minutes.'

'Hey!' Lucy rapped Amy's knuckles as she absentmindedly reached for the vegetables. 'Your dad goes first. Honestly since you fell off that ladder last month you are in cloud cuckoo land.'

'He's not here yet.' She retorted.

'Yes, he is,' the voice came from behind her and went to the butler sink to wash his hands. 'How are my girls then? Oh, one missing,' He and Lucy exchanged glances. 'Simons *again*? Better start then before it gets cold.' Tussling his daughter's curls as he sat next to her a small, tired sigh escaped him. Jess was hardly ever here now and he wished Lucy and Amy had a better relationship but they always seemed to be on the wrong side of each other. As for the wedding plans, he'd never seen one arranged so fast! Was Jess in the family way? No, that much he was sure of. His girls had been brought up right. But once the kids decided to get engaged there had been no stopping his wife and Kate.

'Why wait? And May is such a lovely month for a wedding.' Lucy added, with a conspiratorial smile.

The church was booked, the hall hired, then cancelled. Hold it at the farm he suggested, big barbeque. Lucy was busy getting flowers ordered, she had dresses to make, which was why the lounge looked like a giant marshmallow. That didn't go down well when he said it. The vicar, who had christened the twins, was arranged. Blah blah blah he tuned out frequently, not that he wasn't delighted, his little girl a bride, but well, they were so young and they had so many more choices these days, oh well, what did he know, all best left to the women. Except the bill. He had also arranged the local pub to supply barrel or two. Simon's uncle was being DJ. Apparently, this would involve a *lot* of power cables from the house, he hoped they wouldn't get a power cut. Hay bales were to provide seating and tables, with cloths on them, and the buffet was to be provided by Amy's boss, at a hefty discount, she really liked Amy, which he knew Lucy found hard to fathom but she was also pleased that her youngest daughter was a different girl at work. Women, he would never understand and, living with three of them only seemed to make it harder. When Mona offered to make the cake, he could not *believe* the chorus of "NO." This had, he noted, quickly been softened by adding, "we just want you to come and enjoy yourself." Amy, he chuckled, Amy was providing the cake apparently, she was making it all by herself, at work. When he had choked on his tea, she had put her hands on her hips and screamed, "just because I don't wear dresses or like make up doesn't mean I can't do…stuff!" and off she had stropped. Again. This week she had been making little cakes as a practice for the real thing and, if they were anything to go by, she could have a nice little income making cakes for people. They were selling well in the shop too, so he was told. He sighed, washed up his cup and went back out to the barn.

Amy had other things on her mind. She still hadn't told anybody about her "problem", and the idea of a little accident was still in her head. When she had slipped on the tiled floor at work she had hoped that would be the end of it. No such luck. Despite checking every hour for days afterwards. Everyone was really sympathetic as she limped round, grumpy as hell, but they didn't realise the real reason. She stood up after her dinner and left her surprised parents staring at her still full dessert bowl. It was her favourite.

'I just don't know what has got into that girl.' Lucy stated.

'I suppose there is a lot of attention on Jess, perhaps we should arrange some sort of treat? Just for her. What do you think?' he asked as he stood up, using his subtle way of throwing the responsibility back to her.

Out in the barn Amy started her bike and shot off down the drive, not even stopping to do up her helmet and making Barney jump out of the way, as she flew past the gate to house, the lights shining out in the dark looked way too homely for her liking, she revved a little bit harder and rode off into the dark. She rode along going over her options, and not one of them included *actually* being a mother. Rounding a bend, the torch light coming towards her. Too fast. A bit more concentration. She saw the wall of the bridge as it loomed up, too late she applied the brake, the bike skidded, then… everything went black.

Chapter Seven

'Amy? Honey? It's okay. You're okay.' She was hearing her dads voice but it was distorted by pain. What had happened to her? Where was she? Her leg? She couldn't feel it. She flicked her eyes open, OW! Bright lights! She looked along the bed and saw her leg was up in traction then down to where her hand was being held and stroked as a blurry image of her father appeared, bit by bit. The hand squeezed a little tighter. 'It's alright sweetheart, you're going to be okay,' he paused and quietly added, 'so is the baby.' The concern in his voice, on his face was too much.

Amy sobbed and, as he gently held her, she told him everything.

Almost everything.

He was struggling to understand how, how *could* this have happened? She was still his little girl. He was relieved? No. Yes, honestly. He *was* relieved when Lucy walked in the room. 'Right I'll leave you to talk, um, girly stuff.' He hugged Amy, 'I'll be back soon.' With his shoulders sagged only a *tiny* bit, he left. He agonised over how he was going to tell Lucy? Then decided. He wasn't.

'So, Amy,' Lucy fussed over the bed, avoiding eye contact, 'how do you feel darling, are you in any pain?' She looked at Amy, the dark circles obvious under her eyes. 'Do you need anything?' She placed a hand on the sheets, over the girls' tummy. 'We know about…' she patted the covers.

'Dad said.' She couldn't say much more. She felt embarrassed, tired, confused. It was all too much. She turned her face away.

'We aren't cross Amy,' she tried to smile, 'we wanted to be grandparents. It's exciting. Just not quite how or when we expected. Babies are like that though, unpredictable.' Her mum still looked a little sad, worried?

'What else is it Mum?' Was she *really* OK? Amy worried.

'Amy, I'm sorry, truly sorry, but the person involved? It was Dave Camber.' Lucy paused as Amy took in a breath. 'He didn't make it. I know you were friends…' she tailed off. 'Amy was he, erm was he…'

The hysterical laughter that escaped from the girl in the bed worried Lucy so much she called for sedation.

Chapter Eight

It was the middle of March and unseasonably warm when, 'MUM...MUUUM!' Amy was bent double in the garden, the broken milk bottle and its contents spread all around her. Blood mixed in with the spreading liquid. Jess came down the stairs two at a time, and she and her mother arrived together, closely followed by Dan, who had been in the barn.

'Call the ambulance. NOW Dan!' Please, no, no, she prayed, not yet, it's too soon. With the family history she had plenty of images of still births etched in her head.

'Right.' He mumbled and went in the house to find the phone leaving Lucy to move Amy from the mess on to the wall.

'And you,' she looked at the horrified Jess, 'can bring me cushions, and a blanket.' Taking control was always her forte if her family were in a crisis. As she wrapped Amy and lowered her to the cushions, she hugged her tightly.

It was amazing everyone said that she *had* carried this far, Amy knew, but for herself she couldn't believe she had been so *unlucky*. She couldn't feel anything for the...this ...parasite inside her. It was all wrong...on so many levels.

'Muum, it hurts...so much,' she hugged herself and her mother sat behind her on the ground, rubbing her back.

'Not long now.' They could hear the sirens in the distance, coming closer. After what seemed like hours, that was actually only about five minutes, the ambulance pulled into the yard and two, slightly harassed, blue and black attired men got out.

'Sorry, sheep!'

Dan looked at Lucy, 'Go, GO.' She waved him away.

Dan, who had been planning to fix the stone wall that morning was going to call their nephew to help but the sheep had beaten him to the repair.

'Aren't you a little overdressed for this?' Amy managed before another sharp pain caught her. 'AAHH.'

They checked the cut on her leg, no glass in it, ran a quick bandage round it then went to help her stand. 'Alright, lovely, let's get you on board. You do realise that the waters…?' The smaller one looked at Amy.

'Well, I didn't think there was that much milk in one small bottle!' She retorted before the gas and air took effect. Amy on the stretcher, was mumbling for her dad. In the hospital she woke just enough to see him at the bottom of the bed and then slipped into a welcome, drug induced oblivion.

Amy's eyes flickered open. The familiar white lights above her head caused her to squint. At least this time she knew where she was. Her hand instinctively slid down to the bulge in her tummy and …It was gone! She moved around and felt an uncomfortable prickling sensation. Slowly she raised the covers and peered down. A large white dressing was across her midriff and, she could see her feet! The relief washed over her, it was *gone*. She laid back on the stiff pillows and cried so hard it hurt her tummy before she drifted into semi-consciousness. She was laying on her side when the door opened, with her back to it she couldn't see who it was and feigned sleep.

'Amy, Ames? its only me.' Jess whispered.

She heard her sisters voice but stayed still, not ready to face any of them yet. She knew they were all out there. Waiting. The door quietly closed.

It opened again, this time very loudly and quickly.

'Now then young lady,' a brisk bossy voice with firm footsteps approached the bed, the chair was scraped aside and a wheelchair was soon in its place. 'Time to meet your daughter.' Click, click went the footrests, Amy felt the covers being roughly pulled off of her. 'Your chariot awaits.'

Trying to turn away, Amy winced in pain, her hands went to her plaster.

'OOH. Fiddle, fiddle.' The nurse, any vestige of patience having faded entirely, continued 'your daughter is in an incubator and she *needs* her mother.' The arms were folded and she stared defiantly at the girl in the bed.'

Me too, thought Amy. This startled her, it was the first time she had not automatically wanted her father. She got in the chair and, as she was wheeled through the door, her parents rushed over to her. 'Darling,' her mother stroked her cheek, 'she is *so* tiny.'

'She has a lot of black hair!'

Amy recoiled. Mike had dark hair, she shuddered. Mistaking it for cold, Jess wrapped her in a blanket.

'I hope she loses that, we only have blondes and redheads in this family.' Joked her dad.

'Don't worry even blondes can be born dark haired, it soon changes.' The all-knowing Lucy added.

The nurse briskly wheeled Amy off in the direction of the special baby unit, leaving the others not knowing if they should follow. Lucy gave a tiny shake of her head. Amy should meet her daughter alone.

Amy stared through the plastic container that held the baby, she couldn't think of it as *her* baby, this lifeless thing, connected to drips and tubes and wires. She couldn't *feel* anything. Not even that feeling when she held the new-born lambs? Something…helpless. But they weren't 24/7…and *they* left.

'You can put your hand through that little hole there to touch her.' A nurse pointed it out. 'She won't be in there for long, just a few days while we make sure everything is working as it should.'

Amy turned to face her. 'Do you mean she might…die?' She gulped.

'No, no. Nothing like that.' The nurse replied quickly and gave her a reassuring pat. Amy turned her head, so the nurse didn't see the disappointment in her eyes. Babies were boring, she just wanted to be back out on her bike.

The family arrived silently and stood behind her. She felt her mother's hand on her shoulder and saw the worry in the three faces reflected in the glass window beyond the incubator.

'Being a mother, darling? It's instinctive, stop trying to fight it Amy. We are all here. We will *all* help you.' As Lucy spoke, Amy watched Jess as she shook her head enthusiastically.

'It'll be fun, good practice for when it's my turn.' She grinned at her sister.

Amy looked at the them all, surrounding her with love, her mum, dad and Jess, her beautiful perfect and kind sister/best friend rolled into one and had never felt …so alone.

Chapter Nine

'Waa, waa, waa.' Screams, snot, dribble and hiccups filled the room. Sophie was *really* on one this morning. It was two weeks after coming home and, with little or no let up, Amy had had enough of it. When Lucy, standing in the doorway watching, saw just how bad it was she came over and scooped up the tiny baby.

'Your dad could probably do with a hand this morning, if you think you're up to it?'

Amy didn't need asking twice.

'Now you,' she expertly jiggled her granddaughter to make her giggle, 'how about bath playtime?' She was rewarded with a wide smile and lots of dribble bubbles. She went to the sink and ran some water then retrieved the little yellow rubber ducks from the shelf, hidden so Barney wouldn't steal them. When Jess entered a few minutes later there were soap suds and rubber ducks all over the floor. She grabbed the mop and proceeded to make silly faces at the niece she adored.

'It is lovely to see you back out here, darling.' Dan gave his daughter a playful tug on her hair. 'Not everyone can be a natural parent you know?' His understanding smile edged up his face and caused crinkles round his eyes.

Amy realised he had aged. Was it overnight? 'Sounds like the voice of experience.' This was a little sarcastic, but Amy knew she and Jess were their parent's absolute world.

'When you and Jess were born, after all the other losses, I have to say I was terrified! Besotted, but scared senseless, one would have been scary, but two! I suddenly had a big responsibility for not just one person but three of you? Was I really ready for that? Everyone goes through the nervousness, love, some are just better at hiding it, I guess!

Amy knew her dad meant well but surely, he of all people, must understand there was more to it than a little baby blues. The way Sophie got here, she couldn't just put it behind her, even if she wanted to. It stared her in the face every time she looked at her daughter. A sudden, strange sound behind her caused her to turn.

'Dad…Dad? Are you ok?' she looked at her father as he doubled up and then, to her horror, slid to the floor, unresponsive.

'Come quick,' Amy breathed out, hard. 'It's Dad!'

The sound of a plate breaking on the tiled floor as Lucy dropped, literally, what she was doing and ran into the yard. She headed for the barn, skirted round Barney, who was asleep in the gateway, not caring about the mud that splashed up her legs from the overnight rain.

'Stupid dog.' Lucy shouted crossly, Barney cocked an ear, this wasn't his usual treatment, he got up and trotted after her to the small barn.

Amy arrived, seconds after her mother, to find Dan against a haybale, clutching his chest.

'I have *really* bad indigestion Luce, could I have a Rennie?' He tried to stand.

Lucy took one look at the pale skin, sheen of sweat on his face and the way he kept rubbing his left arm. In a calm, reassuring, firm voice, she took control.

'Stay still.' To Dan. To Amy she said, 'go back to the house and ring an ambulance.'

'But…'

Do it NOW, Amy.' Lucy sat next to her husband. To Dan she said, 'you'll be just fine,' as she rubbed his hand. The confidence in her voice was betrayed by the tiniest of sobs, inaudible above the sounds of bleating lambs and ewes, wondering why they hadn't yet been fed.

Click, whir, woosh, click, whir, woosh, again and again and again it repeated. Lucy sat holding Dan's hand as he slept the constant, rhythmic pattern of the machines was driving her slowly insane. It was a constant reminder of how ill he really was but also of the hope she clung to that he was still with her. The past few days had been hell for her. The loneliness as she watched her childhood friend come husband, unconscious and barely breathing was indescribable. They told her yesterday that he should be out of the woods now but the next couple of days would be vital.

Beeeeep, beeeeep, beeeeep…

The team crashed through the door in seconds and she was, none too gently, pushed out of the door, only able to peer, helpless and afraid, through the glass panel, watching as the professionals worked with chaotic precision on Dan, whilst sending up pleas for him to make it.

As she watched she could not, *would* not, allow the thought of life without him to enter her head.

Fight Dan, please, fight…for all of us.

Chapter Ten

'What is it with this family and hospitals. Honestly if I ever have to see another one it will be the bloody finish of me.' Lucy, in an uncharacteristic outburst, spoke to her sister, who was at the other end of the bunting they were trying to hang across the lounge. The welcome committee for Dan was a small one, so as not to tire him out. Mona and her son had come of course. The boy had stepped in with Amy and learnt the ropes of farming far quicker than anyone had thought possible. He was quite the natural farmer and Lucy felt he should stay on when Dan was back. He had been in the hospital for a month and had been a quite dreadful patient. Lucy had warned him, that when he finally came home, he would do as she instructed or else he would be going straight back in! She knew nothing would ever be good enough for him but the place was ticking along just fine. All she cared about at the moment was getting him fit to walk Jess down the aisle. He was NOT missing out on that. The poor girl had thought she would have to postpone it all. Over her dead body she considered. That thought was quickly followed by a guilt trip, after all, it had nearly been over Dan's.

'Mum look,' Amy appeared, happy, exhausted and filthy, lamb in one hand, bottle in the other, 'she's finally feeding.'

The lamb had been quite a cause for concern, rejected by its mother, so Amy had been up all night with it. Why oh, why wondered Lucy could she not look after her own child with that amount of care. Just then Jess appeared in the doorway with Sophie asleep over her shoulder. She should have been the one to have a baby, she was a right little mother, that one. No amount of nappies, tears or even screaming seemed to faze her. You'd think *she* was the little girls' mother. Simon wasn't quite so enamoured she'd noticed but then he *was* still a boy really, despite getting married in a few weeks. The first seeds of doubt were swiftly pushed aside, after all, they would be living at the farm so between her and Dan they could steer the newly-weds in the right direction, she was absolutely certain. She gave a warm smile to both her daughters. They were each so lovely in their own ways, and despite both still needing their mother's guidance, Lucy felt so very proud of both of them.

'They're here.' Mona called out and the five girls went out to the front yard to meet their men, who were taking it in turns to hug Dan and help him inside. Lucy went first and started making tea as her family trooped back inside. When Dan was settled in his comfy armchair, with Sophie on his lap, Lucy was confident in the knowledge that Dan would soon be back to his old self. They had so much more to look forward to in the years that lay ahead, she was certain.

'Well what do you expect? She was always hanging around with all those boys, I hear Mrs Emsworth packed that young Michael of hers off to another county, just in case there was any suggestion…you know…well, with them being such a well-off family, just the sort that someone would try to pin *that* on.' The customers turned as one as the bell on the door jangled.

'Have you seen the advert? In Appleson-Wright? Mr and Mrs *Mucks*worth. Up for sale. Already gone apparently. Didn't want a scandal. Too good for us round here.' Added the breathless voice behind them.

Nodding solemnly in agreement, the second woman added, '*Her* parents should have known better of course. Hanging around with boys all the time. There's a name for that sort of girl.'

'Yes, it's called unlucky.' Lucy, previously unnoticed behind the shelving had caught the tail end of this exchange, she might not be overjoyed herself but she'd be damned if *her* daughter was going to be the subject of small-minded village gossip.

The women looked only slightly embarrassed. 'Yes, well, was there anything else.' Asked the shopkeeper as she rang up Lucy's purchases.

'Not today thank you.' Not ever, if there was another shop within spitting distance. She picked up her purchases and left knowing that, unfortunately, there wasn't.

Chapter Eleven

'OW! That bloody hurt!' It was a lovely sunny day at the end of May and Amy squirmed as pins were pushed in, hair was pulled up and, it felt like, pulled out.

'If *you* hadn't cut all your hair off, *I* wouldn't need to put this hair piece in.' The hairdressers' patience was starting to run a little thin as she held the rapidly deteriorating piece of fake hair. And it would help if there was something to clip it to!'

'Yes.' Jess interrupted. 'You are NOT being my bridesmaid looking like a bloody boy!' The warm room was getting to all of them.

Amy, surprising herself, bit back the retort about not wanting to be a *fucking* bridesmaid, having to dress in *fucking* taffeta *and* have her *fucking* hair pulled out, just to look good in Jess's *fucking* photo album.

'Now, if you just,' tug, 'stay,' tug, 'still, it will be a lot quicker.' She sighed loudly. 'I still have to do your mum and your sister, you know, *the bride*!'

Jess stood in the middle of the room as the hairdresser fiddled, pulled and poked her hair and her mum tugged and tucked her dress.

'Jess,' her mum choked back tears, 'you look stunning, just like a model, I can't believe you are *my* little girl.' Lucy hugged her, then quickly let her go. 'Mustn't crease the dress.' Jess smiled nervously and went through the door, as she reached the top of the stairs, everyone heard Dan. 'Who are you? And what have you done with my little girl.' The pride evident in his voice. 'I'm sure it was only last week you bouncing on my knee!'

Upstairs Lucy turned to her younger daughter, 'Amy you look so pretty,' she reached out a hand to move a stray strand of hair, but Amy pulled away. Hiding her pain, Lucy looked down into the cot, 'Sophie! don't you just look so cute.' The baby giggled. She had a pretty cream dress on, the consensus was that navy blue was too harsh for one so tiny, It was still the same design as her mothers with a matching headband. They all knew it wouldn't last five minutes so Dan was going to take a quick photo before Lucy took charge of her for the ceremony. Amy watched the two of them go, the usual feeling of relief flooding her. The bonding she was supposed to have? It was still nowhere to be seen.

'I Do.'

'I now pronounce you…'

Amy switched off then. That was it, her closest ally was gone. From now on it would be Simon first, forever. Had been for some time if she was honest. Simon and Sophie. Jess revolved her life around the both of them. Their mum talked of nothing but the wedding or Sophie's development, each inch or ounce a major milestone. No one would notice if *she* dropped dead. For the next hour she smiled, preened and generally behaved as she was expected to then, once the photos were done, the speeches were over and everyone had gone back to the farm to feast on the buffet, she had slipped away, into the woods, still in her bridesmaid dress and shoes.

She kicked these off, carrying them in one hand as she wandered through the cool, shady paths, not caring about the dress being dragged through the dust and snagged on the brambles. She just wanted - needed – to be away from the joviality, the noise. Sophie was well taken care of, the family were playing a game of pass the parcel with her. What exactly was so great about babies anyway? Her whole family were bloody obsessed! She thought they were overrated, noisy, smelly little things. Hearing a noise, she looked across the small pond and saw a bike coming down the track, realising it was Tony Hodder she changed her route. She started to shake and knew it wasn't the cold, taking a path to her left she carried on with her walk.

The music was playing and several people were up dancing now the first dance was over. Even Dan was having a go at Dad dancing with a few of his mates but Lucy was keeping a check on his alcohol consumption, much to his annoyance.
'It's only my second one.' He threw his arms wide.
'What, this hour?' Lucy scowled.
'Aww, Luce, not today.' He pleaded.
Aww Dan…NOT today or any day. I don't need another ambulance here thank you.' Lucy turned at a tap on the shoulder leaving Dan free to escape.
'Doesn't she look lovely?' Bessie Clampett, the village spinster told Lucy. 'You must be so proud.' Then, she lowered her voice to a whisper, 'shame about the other "business".'

Lucy looked across to where Dan was now holding Sophie.

'I must go, I have a sudden urge to give my beautiful, perfect little granddaughter a huge cuddle. Who knows you might have one of your own, one day. Then you'll understand.' Lucy turned away stage whispering, 'no, much too late for that.' She strode off head held high. No was spoiling today. *NO ONE*.

'DAAAD, HELP'. All eyes were on Amy as she ran, across the small field towards the crowd milling around at the back of the farm, the shiny material, now sodden and stained with shades of brown and green. The shoes long discarded.

Dan was almost knocked back as Amy ran into him, all eyes on them.

'Amy, Amy, what on earth?' Dan stroked her hair and looked down at her.

'I…it's… I tried,' her breath came in in short, sharp gasps, 'I did try…he…he's, oh Dad I think he's dead!' The crowd now gathered around them gasped as one.

'WHAT! Who, Amy what happened?' Dan asked as he pushed her back away from him.

'I came around the bend, by the pond, he, he's lying there, face down…there was *blood*.' She held out her hands which were a muddy, rusty colour. She buried her face back in his chest, tears causing streaks down her dirty face, as several of the men made their way down to the woods.

Three men carried the body out of the pond. The boy was face down in the water when they arrived, a rock was under his head, congealed blood on the side of his face, a bike was laying further out in the deeper water.

'Looks like he hit a root and flicked over into the pond.' Jim Sanders, a local builder, was used to seeing accidents so he had taken charge of the first to arrive. When PC Manson took over he called for an ambulance and the local GP was summoned, but it was far too late. No one was sure if the boy died from a hit on the head or had inhaled water when unconscious but that was for another day. The PC left to inform the parents.

Everyone went back to the party but the mood was spoiled and it finished about an hour later. It may have been a tragic accident but, the boy was known to all of them, so the happy atmosphere was tainted.

Simon's dad dropped the couple off at the train station as Dan was still unable to drive and Simon still hadn't passed his test, that pleasure would be next week. They were going to the coast for a long weekend. A treat from Simon's parents. At least they were getting away from here. Amy watched from the bedroom window, staring out into the dark. The tiny hint of a smile strayed onto her lips.

Chapter Twelve

Lucy spent the rest of the weekend making the spare room into a habitable space for the newlyweds to use whilst Dan and Barry worked on converting part of the farmhouse into a small one bed house for the couple to start them off. It had been agreed by the four parents that, at their young ages, the couple should have help at hand to get them the best start, that way they all agreed, the young ones could save up for their own place and hopefully start a family of their own, all in good in time. She put up new lilac curtains and a crisp white cover onto the bed. A fluffy rug was shaken and laid beside the bed and Dan had painted the wardrobe, chest of drawers and a small bedside table in a matching shade of cream. The walls were freshly whitewashed making the whole room fresh and clean. Lucy added a vase of freshly picked pink and white stocks, opened a gap in the window, then shut the door as she saw the taxi pull up. Her daughter climbed out of the rear and did *not* look the happy, radiant newlywed she had been expecting. Simon was paying the driver and went to the boot to retrieve the luggage. She saw them have an exchange, hands waving, then they both turned to the door, smiles fixed in position. Oh dear. It seemed like the honeymoon was well and truly over.

'Sophie!' Jess sounded really excited to see her niece and Lucy walked in to see she had taken the little girl out of her pram and was hugging the baby, a bit too tightly, if the expression on her granddaughter's face was anything to go by.

'Hello darlings, welcome home, Simon if you take the case up, I'll put some tea on. Journeys can be very tiring, can't they?' She smiled at them both and when Simon had turned away, she winked at her daughter. 'We can even rustle up some cake. Your sister is a whizz in the cake department. It's amazing.' Amy's other domestic skills were non-existent, she had happily taken a back seat with Sophie despite Lucy's constant alternating irritation and gentle cajoling. Amy was, however, alive when dealing with the animals, the machinery and the yard. Her two daughters were like chalk and cheese and she was glad Jess was back to rebalance the atmosphere. There hadn't actually been any major arguments the last few days but Amy had been keeping out the way and Lucy had been biting her tongue, *a lot*! With Dan still recovering Amy had been exceptional really, her and her cousin. Now *he* really was a godsend. Deep in thought, she was surprised as Jess came up behind her and gave her a hug.

'Mum.' She squeezed her.

Lucy saw tears in her daughter's eyes, but she just hugged her back, she didn't want to be seen to be an interfering mother-in-law. Especially with them under her roof. It would no doubt sort itself out soon enough.

Summer passed with the harvest uneventful. The weather had been kind, which was a godsend, leaving Dan with less to worry about, it also gave the trainee a gentler introduction into another season of the farming calendar. The harvest festival was a plentiful affair and Lucy and Dan gave thanks with the rest of the village for another successful year of bounty.

'Are we going to help this year? Or is it time to let some younger ones take over?' Lucy asked, as she spotted the beginnings of the bonfire on the village green as they returned from a rare shopping trip to the nearest town. Broken pallets, old chairs and furniture were being piled up in readiness for the annual village event.
'What! we are nowhere *near* the time to give it all up. You love doing the soup and hot dogs.' Dan ribbed his wife. In fact, she just liked to see the fireworks, only the pretty ones, not those noisy banging things. It was fortunate that the farm was far enough out for them to not bother the animals.

'Pull harder!' Dan was supervising the others as they erected the tent for the hot dogs, which was currently collapsing on the men inside. On the other side the younger ones were rigging up the wooden rack for the Catherine wheels and setting out the distance between the grounded ones. The safety rope had been erected earlier by the adults, just to be sure.
'I can't get the electric or the gas to work!' Came a shout from the women trying to get the food and drink set up.
Someone cranked a generator. Another body turned on the gas bottle. 'Thanks.' Chorused a bunch of happier voices. At last everything was ready. Even the rain stayed away this year.

'Aww, ooh, ahh.' The collection of villagers were all concentrating on the fireworks in the sky. The bonfire had been lit and hands were warming around it, faces being filled with hot dogs, the smell of onions drifted everywhere, encouraging more hungry bodies and plastic cups of soup were being consumed in an effort to keep warm. Lucy had been surprised to see Amy holding her daughter and pointing to the sky, smiling and laughing. Sophie was such a good baby, she harboured a secret wish that this could be a turning point. A big bang took Lucy's attention skywards; when she looked back Sophie and Amy had disappeared into the crowd. A siren started as she looked back up. She expected it was the usual village kids, drinking too much, probably burnt their hand. There was always one.

Then Jess found her.

'Where on earth *were* you! For gods' *sake* AMY. You are a *mother*. She. Is. Your. Priority.' Dan stood by as Lucy, quite rightly he felt, blew her top at their youngest daughter.

'I'm sorry, I'm really, really sorry. OK? Is that what you want?' Amy had returned to sullen teenager mode and neither of them could be sure if she had grasped the seriousness of the situation.

'Do you realise, she could be scarred for life?' Lucy shouted.

'Oh, don't bloody exaggerate.' Amy retorted.

'Don't use that language-,'

A cough behind them prevented the altercation becoming an all-out war. 'Sophie,' three faces absorbed every word. 'is-,' The blue uniformed nurse tried to explain.

'Yes?' Lucy, tentatively went first.

'Not,' they all held their breath, 'quite out of the woods yet but it is looking promising. Shouldn't be any major lasting damage, she was lucky that someone experienced was on hand to deal with her.' Lucy didn't know how but she would spend her life making up to Mrs Simm the St John volunteer.

'Her hand will recover and the scarring will shrink as she grows. This is the trouble with fireworks, even when they land, is that they can cause damage as they are still hot. Fires are common. Although to pick one up, as in this instance, is unusual, it *is* common for them to land on people. Hair goes up especially well. All that hairspray and sticky gel that's so popular these days.'

'Can we-,' Lucy and Dan asked in unison.

'Of *course,* you can see her. Would you like to stay with her overnight?' The surgeon looked at Amy.

Lucy got in first. 'Yes, I'll stay. Dan,' she turned away from her daughter, 'take her home.' She couldn't even bring herself to speak her name.

Amy was silent all the way home. Dan attempted to mend some bridges. 'You know Amy, your mum, she does…'

'Go on, you just dig in as well then. "she means well, just wants what's best for you", does she? Does she even know what I want? Or what I've been through?' Amy's voice wavered.

'Now you know I left it for you to tell your mum what actually happened. I kept your secret for sweetheart.' He reached out and rubbed her head, 'is that what all this is about, the short hair?' He asked affably.

'Mm. Maybe.' He really had *no* idea did he she thought.

'Do you want your mum to know? Do you want *me* to tell her?' He sounded so concerned that just for a minute she felt like a child again.

'NO!...I just...I don't know what good would it do now? Two of them are dead anyway.' She shrugged. 'Good riddance.'

Dan was taken aback at just how casual she was. Then he saw her shoulders shifting up and down and heard the stifled sobs.

'I only put her down for a second Dad, just to get something out of my bag, it was dark, I just...I didn't think... and now she may be damaged for life. Dad,' she struggled to speak, 'I didn't mean it, I just didn't think...' She stiffened waiting for the inevitable "that's just the problem you never do," but it didn't come. Her dad just breathed out, hard.

'Oh, Amy.' He sighed.

Tonight she thought, she had managed to prove to everyone what she already knew; she was a *totally* shit mother. Why had this had to happen to her, she didn't want this level of responsibility, she didn't even want to be...perhaps it was time to talk to someone.

Chapter Thirteen

'We are grateful Dad, but by the time Simon gets back he is tired. The course work is really hard and-' Jess was interrupted.

'That doesn't explain why you can't help with the washing up, now does it?' His eyes danced as he threw a tea towel at his elder daughter.

'Aw Dad. We are both excited about the conversion it will be nice to have a bit of our own space. But we are quite happy to carry on eating with you all.'

'I'll bet you are. Your mother must teach you to cook some stuff you know, then perhaps you could take it in turns. Don't look like that you will need to feed your man.' Dan rubbed his own tummy to emphasise the point.

'Oh, I thought that all his promotions should keep us in meals out. Meeting at the pub for a meal after work each night.' She replied airily.

'You're supposed to be saving for a deposit.' Dan looked serious for only a minute, he knew how hard they were squirrelling away.

'A couple of years should do it, with what you and Mum and my in-laws are giving us. We are rather lucky. We like those little starter homes over the other side of the woods. I have been in for a look with Kate.' She sounded old and sensible but that was her way, and he was well aware that she couldn't *wait* to have her very own little Sophie. Simon wanted to wait till they were out of the starter home, he had something he termed as a five-year plan. He was so like his father, an accountant, very solid and dependable.

December 1995 was a happy affair. Lucy had her whole family under one roof, Sophie was starting to toddle and all that remained from the injury was a little scarring on her hand which, they had been assured, would vanish as she grew. Jess and Simon had seemed to settle down. Dan was recovering well, able to drive again now but they had still kept Mona's son on to help and Dan was enjoying teaching him the ropes. Amy, though, was still a worry. She now seemed to have taken umbrage over her cousins help, she had always been daddy's girl, helping with farm, learning the mechanics of the machines and going to the sales with Dan. She was happiest when she had been out to the market. Now, Dan felt, she should be concentrating on her own daughter, but Amy still had other ideas and whenever Dan tried to push her indoors, she was only interested in the kitchen. Lucy couldn't really moan as she was actually a great little cook. Her only saving grace in the domestic department it seemed, but they both wished she would spend more time with Sophie. Jess, on the other hand, loved being with her and Lucy hoped that she wouldn't have an "accident". She knew Jess wanted to be a mother, she took all the noise and mess in her stride, Lucy and Dan wanted them to have a "proper" start to their life. If things were anything to go by they were saving like mad. Going out once a month to the pictures and once a week for one drink at the village pub. Although they were too young to drink, they played pool and caught up with friends. Simon was always a bit quiet when they returned home but, by the morning he was tucking into breakfast with the rest of them and then shut himself away for the morning to study. He wanted promotion and, give him his due, he was working very hard for it. One night a week he was late, attending night school and recently it had turned into two. Dan and Lucy were pleased Jess had found herself with a hard worker. Sometimes Dan, Lucy, Kate and Barry would join them, getting their offspring an extra drink so they could stay a bit longer. On these occasions Sophie was left in the care of her mother. She was always asleep when they left but, after they arrived back one night to Sophie screaming the place down, she was wet, with Amy holding her head in her hands on the sofa, these outings became scarcer.

'Someone pass me the fairy.' Lucy spoke to her family, sitting round the lounge on Christmas eve. Dan was sitting in the large comfy armchair, resting after dinner, before going back for a quick check on the stock. Jess and Simon were upstairs wrapping presents to add to the colourful pile already under the tree, there were raised voices earlier but it was all quiet now. Sophie was getting very spoiled but everyone else just had a small gift each. There had been a storm threatened and all week he had been checking and fixing the wooden barns. Tasks that had been delayed a bit by his spell of recovery had taken on a new urgency and Lucy worried about a repeat bout. He did *seem* to be taking it easier though.

Right, I will be back in a minute.' Dan eased himself out of the chair.

'I'll come with you Dad.' Amy shot to her feet.

'Nah, it's okay love, I'll just be a minute. Here,' he passed her the fairy, 'help your mum.'

'Put the kettle on I'll need a warm drink after being out there.' He said to no one in particular.

Amy made them all a cup, cut a slice of the Christmas cake she had won in a local raffle and waited in the kitchen for her dad to come back. It wasn't one of hers but had been made by her boss as every year to raise funds for the scout group. Though she only worked part time now, Amy was on good terms with Lorna and her boss was always willing to give her extra hours.

'It is actually very calm out there. Still we know that can change in a blink. I'll sleep light tonight.' Dan sipped his tea as Lucy started to set up the Aga. She liked to put the turkey in really early and would be up with Dan before dawn tomorrow. Christmas was always a long day but she never noticed, in her element with the food, drink, family, jollity, she loved every single minute of it. And her little Sophie would make it very, very special this year. She said up a silent prayer of thanks kissed Dan and snuggled down under the covers. Another perfect family day to look forward to, she went to sleep a happy, contented woman.

CRACK.

'What the!' Dan leapt out of bed.

'What time is it.' Yawned Lucy.

'About 2.00 go back to sleep, I won't be long.' Dan shoved back the covers, pulled on his trousers and a jumper over his pyjamas. 'Just have to go and check.'

When Dan got downstairs it was to find Amy in wellies, pyjamas and heavy raincoat, heading out the door.

'I was awake and heard the crash it was too dark to see but I think it was that old ash tree. The one you've been meaning to cut down for yonks?'

'It will keep us in firewood for a whole year if it is.' Dan hoped it had saved him a job too. 'Shit!' A sudden bolt of lightning lit up the room and the scene outside.

'It's not just the tree Dad.' Amy pulled the door bolts back. 'The barn must be damaged, there's sheep everywhere!'

They stepped outside, the wind threatening to tear off their coats. They could see the tree across the drive, a bundle of white pressed up against it. Dan hoped that might prevent the sheep going too far. They called Barney and managed to round them up into the yard, putting the van across the entrance to stop them escaping.

Using their torches, they journeyed up the slippery path to the barns. The small one was undamaged so the equipment was fine, the hay barn door was hanging open, a quick check showed it was the hinges come adrift, another job Dan hadn't quite got around to yet. They heaved a couple of bales out to wedge it closed and went over to the stock barn. As predicted there was damage. *Lots* of damage. It was leaning over to the right as they looked at it and, when they pushed their way through the pile of metal fencing that had fallen, they could see the back right end support had snapped, leaving it not only leaning in a very precarious position, but with sparks flashing from the damaged electric cables.

'Stay there Amy I need to… AAHH!' Dan was fighting his way over a pile of the fencing when he slipped and disappeared from view.

'DAD? DAD, are you okay?' Getting no reply Amy started towards the pile when she heard a moan, then her dad's voice came through.

'I'm okay, I think, I may have damaged my ankle, it's wedged, I can't tell.' He was speaking through gritted teeth. 'Go back to the farm and get Jess and Simon, he's not strong but he'll have to help you this time.' The old wood swayed and creaked ominously above them. 'Hurry!'

'I can't just leave you Dad.' Amy started to tug and pull at the top gate, the sound of metal on metal screeched along with the cracking and groaning, as if it was playing a tune. Realising how futile her efforts were on her own she shouted above the din, 'I'll be quick Dad.' Amy was just reaching the house when she heard the creaking and crashing of the barn collapsing. She hammered on the door to wake her mother then shouted, 'HELP!' knowing she would see to everyone else and tore off back to the barn.

'DAAAD…DAAD?' She listened at the edge of the fallen barn. Above the din she thought she could just hear him.

'Amy…Amy are you there?' So quiet he could have been whispering.

'What happened, where's your father?' Lucy was first; chasing the disappearing light, running up the track, seeing the devastation, she clutched herself and whimpered, 'No, no, no, not Dan.'

Amy shook her. 'Mum he's trapped by his foot I heard him, he's alive Mum.' The noise lulled for a minute and Dan could be heard faintly calling.

'Lucy is that you? Get this bloody barn off me!' He tried to put her at ease as Jess and Simon arrived behind them.

'At least it's not raining.' Simon shivered as they all tried to make a clearing to get to the trapped farmer.

'Just the flippin' wind,' added Jess, pushing her hood back with one hand while holding up a plank of wood, 'it's no good, we need more hands.'

'There's no time. We need to get Dad out before-,'

Inside the still standing part of the barn, flashes were coming thick and fast as the cable was being blown around again and again, then… with a huge flash…the barn caught fire…

Chapter Fourteen

The four rescuers could not believe their luck. Seconds after the first flames got hold the heavens opened and, despite the cold, the wind, the rain and the loose cables, they redoubled their efforts at the pile of wood and metal trapping the injured man beneath. Lucy had gone back to check on Sophie, who was actually sleeping peacefully, no sign of having heard the storm. She went back down and put the kettle on. It was three o'clock and she knew there would be no more sleep for her and Dan. The kids could go back to bed but she'd nap in the chair after she put the turkey in.

'Keep still,' Lucy grabbed Dan's leg and made to sit on it. 'I don't think it's broken, just a cut and a bad sprain.' She expertly cleaned, dressed and strapped it up then handed him his tea. She sat down and, suddenly, she couldn't help the tears. Dan put out a hand and she went to him, sitting on his lap like she was a little girl. 'I just don't know what I'd do without you.' She laid a hand over his.

'I do, you are a strong woman my Lucy Lou always knew it, knew I could depend on you and I do, and I still will do for many, many years to come.' He kissed her gently on her salty lips. 'Now get that turkey in the oven, woman and we can have a nap in the lounge,' he winced as he tried to stand, 'do we have any pain killers anywhere?'

The morning started early. Amy called her cousin, who arrived within half an hour to help her make a temporary pen for the sheep in the hay barn. He promised they would start on the barn the next morning and he rang the chippy, who had called straight back to say that he and a couple of others would be over too to help. Lucy made her nephew call them back and invite their families to come with them for an impromptu party. Dan looked at her with admiration.

'Don't think you are going to sit idle. You're going to be helping in the kitchen.' She threw him her best, "I mean it" look.

'But-,'

'Don't bother with the "but", Dan Collier.'

He knew when to concede a defeat, went to get a pinny and put it on, much to her amusement and started cutting up potatoes.

'You have to *peel* them first!' Lucy's eyes were wide in disbelief and laughter.

New year came and went and Amy was getting more and more despondent, she tried to hide it around the family but she was feeling lower and lower. This life just wasn't what she wanted. She wasn't sure exactly what she *did* want, but she did know some of it. And she knew her parents couldn't help her.

'Miss Collier would you come this way please.' The smart looking secretary smiled revealing perfect white teeth and Amy started to feel a little bit self-conscious.

She hadn't been to the local surgery for some time and it had altered. A lot.

'Amy, good to see you,' Dr Mayberry smiled at her.

'This, um, this is secret, isn't it?' She asked before she sat down

'Everything is bound by doctor patient confidentiality Amy.' He replied, a slight frown on his face. 'Is everything alright with you, with Sophie.'

Amy, relieved, sat down and started to speak. Then everything... all of it... just came pouring out, the relief was indescribable. She didn't look at the doctor as she spoke and, when she had finally finished, she looked up to see concern and amazement etched on his features.

'I, erm,' she was embarrassed now. He sensed this and gently explained.

'Amy, it is okay to feel like this, after what you've just told I am almost not surprised. But,'

She let out a deep audible sigh. She knew there would be a "but".

'I just don't *ever* want to have to go through this again.' She was emphatic.

Don't get ahead of me,' he responded. 'There are several issues here, firstly, you are obviously and understandably depressed. Second you may need some counselling for the...' he hesitated, 'attack,' was the word he chose as safest. 'Now as for the other matter, you have a child, but that is still quite a drastic step. I am afraid you are definitely too young for that. I am not sure you are even able to decide that at present.'

'I've always felt it though.' She pleaded.

'That may be so Amy, however you would need to wait at least two more years to even be considered, even then, I doubt it could happen before you were at least twenty-one. There are certain criteria that would have to be met first too.'

'What?' She wasn't letting go now. When Amy left the surgery, twenty minutes later, she absolutely certain of what she wanted and how to achieve it. She just didn't know how on earth she was going to tell her parents, for different reasons, neither one would understand. For the first time she wished she had a girlfriend, or any friend for that matter, that she could confide in, but they had all disappeared when she had shut herself away. She considered Lorna but knew she would just think she was even more weird than she did now. She might even feel she had to tell her mum!

Dan was sorting out the rebuilt barn when Amy arrived back home. Her little scooter could be heard coming well before it was seen and Dan's head appeared out of the door.

'Sounds a bit rough.'

'I know. I'm just going to check it over.'

Dan, unfazed by his tomboy daughter these days, had taught her how to look after the bike, and some other machinery, after she made it very clear that it wasn't just her cousin who could do boy's stuff. In fact, he had to stop himself laughing at the time as she had actually stamped her foot before walking away, just like she had when she was small. He walked in behind her. 'When you're done come and help me with the pens?'

'Hmm,' was all she managed, distracted now, physically by pulling and pushing various parts of the bike, mentally by going over what had been discussed. She turned to say something to him but she saw his back as he walked away.

'Don't you think we should at least try?' Dan said later when they were alone.

Lucy sighed. 'Not again Dan, *I* have tried. *You* have tried. She has got the baby blues and hopefully, at some point, she will get over it and start to behave like a mother. In the meantime-,'

'I know, I know, "we have just got to be patient and supportive". I know what you said Lucy, I just worry that Sophie sees you, or even Jess, as her mother.' He drained his cup. 'At least she is a whizz with the machinery, so she hasn't lost interest in everything.' He shrugged.

'You can send her in to make a cake when you've finished with her. I thought she might have bought one back with her from work. Funny, it's unusual not to.' Lucy frowned, then went back to her sewing. She had started to make little quilts for the spring fete. They sold very well, for cots or cats usually. It was a good way of using up the scraps and the village often dropped bits of curtain material or old clothes. Dan got really annoyed once when the pile got a little larger than normal. "What do they think we are? the local rag man?" It was so unlike him that Lucy had sat up half the night cutting the clothes up, folding and boxing the good bits and taking the excess out to the incinerator. Then she found a space in the cupboard for the, now much reduced, off cuts. When Dan got up in the morning and realised how hard she must have worked he at least had the decency to look a l*ittle* sheepish. Especially when he saw the pile of blue triangles, each one stitched with his initials and "happy birthday", he was less amused when he saw all the little 40s she had made, as if he needed reminding! He knew the party would be brilliant, theirs always were but couldn't the reason behind this one just be toned down a little? Please?

In the yard Amy stood up and wiped her hands on a rag, she always had one sticking out of her pocket, just like her dad. It was a comfort as it always reminded her of him when she used it. She heard whistling and knew he would want to get started in the barn. She wheeled the bike out of the way and went out to meet him. They set about moving some of the bales and fencing around to make space for his party.

'God these are heavy today,' Dan, slightly out of breath now, sat down on a nearby hay bale.

'Showing your age Dad?' Amy laughed as she carried the last panel into position, it slipped into place and she moved out of the way, ready for the bale that her dad was still sitting on. Except, when she turned around, he *wasn't* sitting on it anymore. He was on the floor leaning against it, white and sweaty and clutching his chest.

'DAAD!' Not again…Dan heaved up his chest with an audible intake of breath then he curled up again and, with a whoosh, he exhaled sharply, his head slumped forward, onto his chest then… he was perfectly still.

Chapter Fifteen

The morning of the 14th of February was grey and overcast. Wet and windy weather was forecast all day and, for once, they weren't wrong. Lucy had nearly been apoplectic when she was given that date but, unfortunately, there was still a backlog due to a previous storm causing a landslip which had dislodged the terraces in the graveyard, and the repairs had been difficult. Mona and her husband arrived at the exact same time as Simon's parents, both of whom were giving lifts to the family. The pleasantries and moans about the weather were quickly dispensed with as Amy appeared at the door with, surprisingly, Sophie in her arms. Mona and Kate shared raised eyebrows, until the baby started to scream and Mona, sensing frustration, swiftly went to take the little girl.

'There, there.' She jiggled the baby up and down.

'Mum is really not herself, and I just don't know what to do with her.' Amy blurted out.

Mona had Sophie over her shoulder now and was rubbing her back. The baby let out an enormous burp and fell silent. 'You see,' she directed her comments at Amy, 'it's not that difficult.' As Mona went to hand her back Amy disappeared inside the door and left her, literally, holding the baby. She went in through the open door to find Lucy, who wasn't in the kitchen making tea, nor was there the usual cheery greeting. She didn't like this, it was eerie, so unlike the cosy home she was used to visiting. Moving towards the sitting room the door was ajar, Lucy was sitting, or rather, slumped, in Dan's favourite chair with one of his shirts in her lap twisting it round and round, the birthday decorations still lay in a heap on the table and the present sat wrapped on the floor. She didn't even look up as her sister pushed open the door. The sorry state of her shocked Mona, her big sister, the one she had always turned to for help and advice now needed *her.*

'Lucy?' gently she went to place Sophie on her lap. Lucy didn't move. 'Lucy, love, its time.' Lucy turned away from her. Mona, not knowing what to do went out and called for Jess to take Sophie out to the car with her, then returned to take her sister by the hand and lead her out.

The funeral was a large affair. Dan had been a very popular man, as was Lucy. Today though the new widow shunned them all. Gone was the happy, calm demeanour, in its place a small, weakened form, huddled in a long black coat that appeared two sizes too big, she muttered her thanks to them for coming, seeming not to hear the condolences, her platitudes automatic in response. She was broken. Her rock, her soulmate, her Dan, was gone. He had left her behind, an empty shell.

'That's the last of them.' Amy shut the back of the sheep trailer and spoke sadly to her cousin as the vehicle pulled away. 'Your help has been invaluable you know.' She knew when he first came that she had been jealous, a right bitch actually at times. But he was family, he'd been like a little brother when they were growing up and it was important to her to let him know that none of it mattered. Lucy was still noncommutative, even Sophie's first birthday in a couple of weeks hadn't been mentioned. Normally there would be cakes to make bunting to hang and a whole host of other activities and bustling around the place.

'So, what now?' He was asking Amy but, she was...*crying*? Amy didn't cry. He went to her and hugged her, not knowing what else to do.

'I'm just sad for... for Dad.' She said as she pulled away, embarrassed. She wiped her face into her hands and dirt streaked across it then she turned and went into the house. Ignoring Sophie and Jess on the way in she went straight upstairs, lay face down on her bed and cried, and cried, and cried until she fell asleep.

'AMYYY, AMY get down here this minute!'

Amy bolted upright at the sound of her mother's voice. As she descended the stairs her sister was behind Lucy giving her their "she is really on one" look they used to use as kids.

'What Mum?' she spoke blearily, she knew she had done everything up at the barns and if she had left a gate open, well, it hardly mattered now, did it.

'Don't, "what Mum", me, young lady.'

Honestly this was the most vocal their mother had been for weeks. Both girls stared at her, wondering what was coming next.

'Your sister and I have been taking care of *your* daughter for long enough!'

Both girls started and took a sharp breath.

'Your sister should be at WORK! Saving for a home of her own, NOT looking after *your* child! She will be a year-old next week. It's time you got a grip and took your responsibility seriously. It wasn't *our* fault you let yourself get pregnant.'

Jess looked stunned, while Amy went white, it was true that Jess had left work but it was to look after Lucy and help at the farm. It had also been her own decision. She initially took some holiday and had thought they could all keep the farm going, but Simon wasn't cut out for farming and made it very clear where their life was heading, "and it wasn't on some godforsaken back water in the middle of nowhere". Jess, who at the time had been quite shocked and upset at his outburst, had still been determined to help out, for now.

'Now those bloody animals have all gone you can start concentrating all your efforts on your daughter.' Lucy always referred to "those bloody animals" since Dan died. She needed something to blame. The sheep were the obvious contender, if he hadn't been outside with them, he would never have had the fatal heart attack. In her current state of mind, it was that simple.

'She is your responsibility as of *now*. Jess ring your boss and ask for your old job back, if not, find another one. You and Simon are going to need to get a mortgage next year as soon as you'll both turn eighteen. There are going to be some big changes round here.' Lucy left the room, and after a while, they could hear scraping and bumping coming from upstairs. Not daring to ask what it was they looked at each other for a full minute. Jess spoke first.

'Where did all that come from?'

'Search me.' Amy shrugged. They both knew their mother was still grieving but that scenario had been so out of character. She looked over to where her daughter lay. Nope, still not feeling it.

Jess gave her sister a hug, 'you're still my little sister,'

'Watch it.' Amy pulled back from her sister a grin on her face.

'And, I really don't mind you know,' As Amy gave her sister a puzzled look Jess went on, 'looking after Sophie. I love it.' She watched the little girl pick up something off the floor. 'No, no Sophie.' The baby grinned at her. 'I wish she was mine sometimes.' Wistful now, then, realizing she may have gone too far with that last statement she shot a guilty look at her twin.

Amy muttered, 'so do I.' Then turned away.

'He's going *travelling*?' Lucy nearly spilled the tea she was pouring. It was Easter and the family had descended on the farm as usual. Except it wasn't as usual, there was no Dan, so she had kept it small. It would also have been their 21st anniversary but she was keeping her mind off that one. She had been to the grave and left flowers, couldn't have him thinking she had forgotten, she'd thought as she laid them down. Lucy hadn't cooked today, everyone had bought something for a buffet but Simon's parents still felt awkward around Lucy and had a "prior engagement, you know how it is?" when Lucy rang to invite them. She was quite upset actually as Kate was her oldest friend. Still, her girls were here and Simon, as were Mona, Phil and their two.

'Yes, he mentioned somewhere that sounded like vatman, but then he found out there was a bit of trouble there, so now he is going to, "go where he can, when he can and, do what he can". Apparently. He says the experience he gained here on the farm will be very useful.'

'But our family don't *travel*.' Lucy was incredulous, to her it was unthinkable to be anywhere else but the village where you grew up, or at least within walking distance.

'Talking of moving-.'

'Which we weren't.' Lucy replied 'I told you before, we are fine. There's some money in the bank and old Mr Travers has given me six months reduced tenant rent, while I think about what I want to do. He's also offered the kids one of his terraces in the village to rent, as soon as it comes empty.'

'Yes,' replied Mona, 'I heard old Mr Dawkins was on his last legs,' she pulled a face, 'not the best start in a new home is it?'

'It's the nature of life besides, beggars can't be choosers. A lick of paint and it will be good as new.' Lucy answered.

'Yes, and a de-infestation might not go amiss either…OW.' Mona yelped as Lucy flicked her ear. She hadn't done that since they were kids and, secretly, she was pleased for any sign the old Lucy was returning.

Vietnam? Amy had overheard her mum and aunt Mona chatting. Anywhere? Lucky sod!

'Amy, are you there?' Jess was looking for her sister and had Sophie in tow so she hid behind a haybale and pretended to be asleep. Their conversation at lunch had not gone well. Jess had insisted on dragging up the "unspoken" It seemed that with Lucy's change of attitude Jess thought it fine to muscle in too. Well, it wasn't!

'Why won't you just admit who the father is?' Jess demanded.

'Why won't you all just stop asking?' Amy retorted, sullen now.

'Oh, come on. It's pretty obvious – Sophie's colouring,' contrary to Lucy's opinion the dark hair *had* stayed, 'the way you were always hanging round him.'

'And the others,' Amy pointed out. 'perhaps it could be any one of them? Shall we just throw that into the mix?'

'The way his parents packed him off to the Outer Hebrides?' Jess replied.

'They changed his university, so what?' Amy shrugged her shoulders.

'Don't you think you ought to just admit? At least they could help, financially, I mean. That is what they were afraid of wasn't it? being forced into marriage with an *unsuitable* girl? Nothing but the best for *their* precious darlings. Look at how his sister treated you. It was nothing short of disgusting. I'm surprised they tolerated your friendship with him. Oh, that's right, I almost forgot, they didn't *like* you being in their house did they? You only went there when they weren't in. And what does that leave to the imagination?' Jess was never usually this argumentative but she was on a right roll now. 'Out with it, Amy, you gave it up and you got caught. Big deal, but at least admit the truth.'

'Truth! truth, you couldn't even begin to *believe* the *truth*!' She had slammed out then making Sophie cry, for which she did feel a little bit bad about. Perhaps she should have told her mum what had happened? Could it be any worse? She'd probably think she had asked for it by going along in the first place. Or would she? Maybe, just maybe, it was time for the truth, the whole truth. Once Jess and Sophie had gone, she went out and wandered over to the woods. She sat down and stared into the pond. Or, maybe, not quite *all* of it.

Chapter Sixteen

'*What* did you just say?' the voice was so quiet, so horrified that Amy knew at once she should *never* have told her mother. The sympathy she had had for her daughter had slowly, but finally, slipped away as she finished recounting her story. It had taken her two weeks to pluck up the courage.

'Did your father know about this?' Lucy demanded.

Amy looked at the floor.

'I asked you a question… DID DAN KNOW?'

'He, well…some, he,' The slap came out of nowhere. Hard and fast. Her mother had *never* raised a hand to anyone in her life. The shock left Amy speechless. She stared at her mother, hand to her face which was now stinging. A lot.

'YOU. ARE. DISGUSTING. This, he kept this all in? No wonder he had a heart attack. You were his precious little girls, and you,' she pointed at her, 'you gave him *this* to deal with? GET. OUT. OF. MY. SIGHT. You as good as killed him, do you realise that.' Lucy was fast becoming irrational now. 'DO YOU?' she pushed her daughter aside, not even stopping when Amy fell over, and went into the house, slamming the door shut behind her.

Amy got up and looked after her mother. You are my mother. You were supposed to understand. But Amy knew in heart that her provincial mother would never deal with it. The sheltered life Lucy had enjoyed with

Dan by her side was fast unravelling and Amy's untimely revelation was just a step too much for her to cope with.

She went into the barn and waited till she saw her mother leave for the village. In her bedroom she packed a bag, went into where Sophie lay asleep. After staring at her for a full five minutes, taking in every little feature, every curl in her hair, she bent down and kissed her lightly on the head, stroked her cheek and whispered, 'goodbye, my little one. You really will be better off without me.' One small, silent tear dripped off Amy's cheek onto the baby, causing her to stir slightly, then with a promise that she was never coming back to that house…she was gone.

Chapter Seventeen

The sun was up early on a cloudless morning. July wasn't far away and the farmhouse was a hive of activity. Packing crates, sheets of newspaper and suitcases were everywhere along with tins of paint for the new house.

Simon, as had become usual of late, was nowhere to be seen and Jess and Lucy were loading as much as they could into the two vans. Lucy had by now got used to driving it but she could still smell Dan in there and it always made her a little sad. It was still early days but with Sophie and the move to take her mind off things she managed. Just. There had been no word from her younger daughter, and the one thing she was certain of? Amy would never be mentioned again. God, had she really hardened that much?

Jess had tried and tried to get her mother to explain, but all she would receive was the same response every time.

'Your *sister* is disgusting and Sophie is better off without her.'

This was so unlike her but in the end she and Simon had a life to build so she threw herself into the new house. Many bits of furniture had been donated to them and they didn't want for much at all. Yes, they would need to save and replace it all one day, but for a while, it would just be nice to be in their own home. Although Simon was already talking of the move to the wider world that would come with his promotion one day. Jess took it all in her stride, by the time that happened and they had a little one, or maybe two, in the village where they both grew up she knew that he would agree with her and wouldn't want to take them to some strange city to go to school. No. they would grow up here, go to school here, just like they had, and Jess and Simon could grow old together just like…she stopped herself. She thought of her mum and dad, who had probably thought the self-same thing, all those years ago. Look what happened there. Sadly, she shook her head. It was true, she thought, you could make all the plans you liked, but you never *really* knew what life had in store.

'Hurry up Jess.' Barry was on a schedule, 'I have to get back to work. I'll be round later to give a hand with the painting. Okay?'

'Thanks, I'll have Simon up a ladder by then I expect.'

Her father in law replied with a surprised tone. 'Really?' As he drove off.

She wasn't so sure herself now, as there had been another unfinished row this morning.

'Sophie, NO.' The little girl was sitting by the packed cases pulling out all the clothes they had painstakingly folded, ready for the next charity sale.

'Mine.'

'No, they're not, they don't fit you anymore.' Just then a teddy flew out of the box. It had been Amy's when she was little.

'Mine.' Sophie grabbed it and hugged it to her.

Jess stared sadly at the miniature, dark-haired version of her sister. 'Yes,' she whispered 'I suppose it is.'

A noise behind her startled her. The postman cycled up to them and handed a pile of letters to Lucy.

'Foreign one today. Must be from that nephew of yours.' It was a small place so everyone knew the boy had gone on his travels.

'I except so. Just put them on the table Jess and lock up. I'll read them later.' Lucy was exiting the door, her hands full of curtains. They had been donated and, where Lucy would have normally set to with the machine, Jess had been ordered to alter them.

'I haven't got time at the minute.' Lucy would say, as she sat in her chair stitching the tiny quilts for the fete. She seemed to find it therapeutic, so they all left her to it.

They arrived back at the farm some hours later and Simon had finally joined them, avoiding all explanation of where he had been, so Jess had given up trying. It was, probably, some sort of surprise for her and she didn't want to spoil it. She let it go for the moment as she set about getting tea ready for them all. Lucy sat and opened her letters. She saved the foreign one till last. Tearing open the envelope in anticipation of another bout of tales from her nephew she was surprised to see expensive cream paper. As she unfolded it, a solicitor's name and address appeared at the top. Slowly, she scanned the words, then she re-read it, folded it up and put it back in the envelope. The words, "with regret" and "no more" swam in her head. She went to stand, her legs gave way beneath her and she slid to the floor knowing, for certain now, that Amy would *never* be coming home.

Jess handed her mother a cup of tea. 'I'm so sorry Mum.' She had read the letter and tears spilled down her face. Tears of regret and of anger, why hadn't her sister confided in *her?* come to her? anything, she had always thought her sister could tell her *anything*. It all made sense now. The boys, the falling out, the reluctance to talk about Sophie's father. Surely, she should have felt…something…aren't twins supposed to have that, "cut me and my sister bleeds", thing going on? Sophie. Oh, god what about Sophie? She had always believed that one day Amy would return for her…Now, she never could.

Chapter Eighteen

Lucy looked around the little cottage she and Sophie now called home, the Christmas tree would have to be so much smaller than the one she had been used to in the farmhouse, still she was lucky that this house came free, just in time for her decision to leave the farm in October. Her landlord had allowed her to carry it through to November but the new tenants were antsy to get in, so she had taken this one before he could finish the repairs. But it was no hardship to live through the new plumbing and now it was finished she could get on with the Christmas arrangements. She had given away *so* much stuff but the tree lights were all working and she had kept the fairy safe. She and Sophie were adjusting to a new life and, with Christmas only days away, there was much to do. To be honest she could have done without Christmas, her first without him. She wanted New Year and the, "first year", over and done with. She had Sophie to look after, even if this had been the worst year of her life, she glanced at Sophie, asleep on the sofa. Now she just had to get on with a new start. Jess had given her good news as well, new house, new baby, they knew it was only six weeks, a little early to be getting excited but the family needed some happy news. They were only five doors away too, so she could help her daughter through it all. She sent up a silent prayer that the, "family curse" had skipped a generation and that the new year would be a great year.

'Sophie don't be difficult.' Lucy smiled at herself, did a two-year old even know what being difficult was?

'She'll be fine when you leave,' The playgroup manager said with an, "I've seen it all before" reassurance but Lucy *wasn't* reassured.

'What if she isn't?'

'Look, I've been doing this a long time, believe me, when she gets stuck into the sand pit and sees all the others, she *will* be fine.' The woman smiled and took Sophie off her before she had a chance to say goodbye, adding more gently, 'go and do your job and let me do mine.' Then firmly shut the door.

Lucy was due to start at the new Home over the other side of the orchards, at the far end of the village. It wasn't a new building but an old manor house they used to play in when it was derelict, as children. It was a lovely setting and made a great place for people to recover. As she understood it though most of the "inmates" were there for good, it just sounded nicer to call it a convalescent home rather than a care facility. She was starting a shift as a cleaner today but had also been taken on in the kitchen to make some of her specialities twice a week. As she turned the corner, she realised she had to walk past the old Emsworth house. Unable to stop a shudder she pulled her coat tighter. She actually wished she could have turned back the clock and been firmer about Amy's choice of friend but, at the time it was better than not having any at all and she was only a child. She hurried along a bit faster now, this was her new start, another small step along the road of her new life and she didn't want to be late. She was going to start a savings account later and planned to call into the post office on her way home to start one each for her and Sophie, then when Jess had her baby, she would open one for them too. She planned to put the equivalent of one hour's salary in each child's account every week then, when they turned eighteen, they could have the money. She had done this for Jess and Amy and this year they, she stopped herself, what was she going to do with Amy's money? Their eighteenth was this year. She must pass the money to Sophie. Somehow though, she couldn't bring herself to close the account.

'So, of course I said,'

Lucy tuned out of the conversation that was holding up the queue in the post office. She checked her watch to see how much longer she had till she needed to pick up Sophie. She wasn't going to be left she knew but, after this morning's episode, she wanted to be on time and she was worried about how she had got on without her. It was no good, she would just have to come back tomorrow.

'NEXT.'

Maybe there was just time then. But the transaction took longer than she thought. When she finally rushed out of the Post Office, towards the zebra crossing, a boy was stepping out onto it and she automatically followed. She knew Amy had been friends with him, then she started as she realised, *he* was one of *them.* Her concentration lost, she didn't look both ways before she stepped out…BANG. She heard the noise of flesh on steel. She saw the boy lying in front of her, blood leaking from his head as the back of the car, now wildly out of control, hit *her* too.

'It's been six months Jess how much longer are we going to have to look after her?' Simon moaned again.

Six months. The words were like a slap in the face. That was how far she had got with her pregnancy, lost in mid-May, just after her mums hit and run. Simon's mum had, amazingly, been fantastic and her aunt Mona had come to Lucy's home and taken care of Sophie.

No one could tell her if her loss was caused by the family issue or the shock over her mother's accident but the outcome was the same so she didn't really care too much about the reason. Now they had taken Sophie into their own house but Simon was finding it a little trying.

'What would you have done if ours *had* been born?' It was a low blow but really, Sophie was adorable and what was with him anyway.

'I'm going to Mum and Dads to study.'

'Don't slam-,' CRASH, '-the door.' She sighed. Family was family and Simon would have to get used to it. Lucy was still in a coma and next week the doctors were hoping to bring her out of it. They had been warned not to get their hopes up. Perhaps she would talk to him about their own home. They must have some savings by now, surely?

'Mummy?'

Jess blinked and looked at Sophie. The little girl came over and lifted her arms up to Jess and repeated the query, 'Mummy, up.' She picked up the little girl and sobbed into her hair. She wasn't parting with this little girl for anything. Not now. Not ever. If Sophie thought she was mummy, then that was enough, she was going to be the best ever mummy that a little girl could hope for. Amy, Lucy and Jess…all rolled into one.

The following week the doctor stood tall and solemn in his white coat, holding a clipboard which he constantly referred to and, although he was quite scary to Jess, this was now beginning to irritate her. She squeezed Simon's hand. But he just stared at the woman on the bed. The various tubes were busily being removed by three different nurses. Suddenly the room was silent and empty.

'Are you ready?' The doctor looked at her and waited for her to respond.

Jess managed a tiny nod. The doctor pressed a switch. It seemed like a lifetime but Lucy's chest started to rise with very shallow breaths. Jess hadn't realised she had been holding her own breath until she let out an audible sigh.

'Shouldn't she, erm, open her eyes?' Simon queried.

'One step at a time.' He spoke gently. 'That is just the first move. We need to monitor for brain activity and tomorrow, all being well, we *may* see some signs of recovery. Take some comfort, she is breathing on her own and that is a very good indicator for the future.'

As they watched her eyelids flickered and Jess could have *sworn* she heard her mother whisper, "Amy" then a few seconds later, "Dan". The doctor looked up suddenly then back down as he hastily scribbled some notes. Jess couldn't fathom it. Surely, speaking of the dead could not be a good sign.

Lucy was sitting up when Jess came back the next morning. Mona was already there fussing over her. But the news was not great.

'I am afraid there is some, probably permanent, brain damage.' Behind him Jess could hear her mum's insistent voice,

'But I *did*. I know what I saw, Amy *was* at the end of the bed. I knew she'd come home. And,' she was nodding, 'and she had Dan with her.' Her head was nodding faster now, so sure was she, of what she had seen.

Jess's eyes filled up and she was having trouble focusing on the doctor's words. She moved over to the bed so she could hold her mum's hand and gently rubbed it as she reminded her. 'Amy is gone Mum, remember? so is Dad?

'NO. No I…they were…' Lucy looked to her sister as she pointed to the end of the bed, Mona moved her head, almost unseen, and Lucy rolled over and wailed into the pillow, over and over.

'No. No. Nooo.' Until the cocktail of drugs kicked in.

Chapter Nineteen

'I won't be gone long!' Simon's voice carried across the room as he packed his case.

'Right NOW? Can't it wait?

He turned to face her. 'NO. Jess, it can't *wait*! It's what I have been training and studying for!'

'Why does it have to be so far away?' She wailed.

His patience was running out now and he ran a hand through his hair as he continued. 'They only do the interviews at head office and they only do them twice a year. I would have to wait another six months-,'

There was that bloody timeline again.

'-before I can try again.' He grabbed his case off the bed and hauled it downstairs. 'Now I *have* to go. The Taxi is waiting.' He looked out of the window.

'And WHY do you have to travel up there with *her*?' Jess was getting very pissed off now.

'I told you, the firm is covering the costs and we are both being put forward for a promotion. It's a big company, there are lots of openings.' He gave her a very quick peck on the cheek and left the door open on his way out.

She wasn't sure if that was better or worse than slamming it. She shut it and leant against the back of it. How did they get to here? What had happened to her family? In such a short space of time everything had changed, they were all gone. She knew that Simon and Sophie were the future, her future. She just hoped her mum was going to improve. And her marriage.

'This is the room we have ready.' The kind woman added, 'I'll just leave you for a minute, shall I?'

Jess nodded but couldn't bring herself to speak she stood looking at the sad looking Christmas tree, broken lights and a fairy with one leg. No one bothered much with Christmas here.

'They don't know what day of the week it is let alone which month.' Appeared to be the general consensus.

One member of staff had at least tried to make an effort. It seemed cruel somehow, her mum was supposed to work here, not be *in* here. But at least it was nearby. The brain damage was too extreme for her to be able to go home alone and, with a bit of wrangling by the doctors, the council had got her a place in here. It was familiar to her which, they hoped, would help to calm her. That, and the strong meds. Sometimes she would just fall asleep mid conversation. The doctors believed she would make some more progress but were reluctant to give her a definite prognosis.

'Alright Mum?' Jess asked her. Sophie was toddling along behind and Lucy looked round to see her. Her granddaughter always bought a smile to her face.

'Mmm.' Lucy answered. Her vocabulary was very limited these days. Along with her ability to walk far. She sat in her chair, staring at the clock on the wall, waiting for the visitors that would never come. Even though she asked for them both every day. Each morning she told anyone who listened that today was the day they would be here. Today. She was so used to people coming and going, the quiet was deafening.

Jess said goodbye and left. She was looking forward to that evening at home Simon should finally find out if his promotion interviews had been successful. She couldn't believe how many different visits to the head office had been required and over the last three months she felt he had been away more than at home. He had even shut himself away at his parents, for more study, as it was quieter there! Honestly there was only her and Sophie and she was no noisier than any other child. In fact, sometimes she was so quiet Jess wondered if she was alright. She had kept her at the child minder two mornings a week, just for some peer company, initially, but now she had taken a part time job to supplement her needlework, which was a bit thin on the ground at the minute.

'WHAT! IT'S *WHERE*? Did you know this when you applied? DID YOU?' Jess was fuming and it showed. She had had just about enough now. It was only a week before Christmas and the last few months had taken their toll. Now Simon was getting the full force of it. Mind you, it wasn't without reason. The freshly manicured nails were waved around in fury and her hair, which had been washed and curled to within an inch of its life earlier, part of a special effort for him, what with Sophie, his extra working hours and her mother lately she had felt a little...invisible. And now, this! It was unbelievable!

'NO. I knew there were various openings but…'

'Well, you can't take it can you. You'll just have to wait for a nearer position.'

'Jess, I,'

'What?'

He flinched, 'I accepted…this morning.'

He might as well of slapped her. 'You'll just have to un-accept then, won't you.' Her hands were on her hips now. 'I cannot go halfway up the country just now. You *know* I can't.'

'Jess, I, I…don't want you to.' He started.

'Sorry, you mean you're going to commute? How's that going to work then? Go on Monday come back Friday? What are we supposed to do in-between? Are you going to find us a house to join you?'

'I, erm,'

It was then she saw the suitcase behind the door. Her eyes widened. 'It's her isn't it?' The penny dropped and he at least looked a little guilty.

'I never meant…'

'GET. OUT. NOW.'

'Jess, I.'

'NOW.'

He left in the sleet, leaving the door ajar. The cold wind blowing through the house was nothing compared to the ice in her heart. Jess sat on the stairs, amid the candle light and wept. When the tears and sobs finally eased, she stood up, wiped her face, then, with the black streaks of eye liner across her cheeks and the re-modelled, second-hand, red velvet dress, ruined by the kohl now smeared over it, she took a deep breath, walked to the door and, with a satisfying clunk, locked the door.

PART TWO

Chapter Twenty

'But that's just not *fair* Mummy!'

Here it comes…STOMP…So like Amy, thought Jess for about the millionth time, at 8 years old Sophie was fast turning into a replica of Jess' twin, in all of the worst ways. What had happened to that sweet little girl she had moved out of the village with all those years ago?

'Can't we just all apologise and move on?' The headmaster cast a bored look at the three females across from him.

Sophie just kept getting into trouble. Jess had been called into the school more times than she could think of this year, but this time it really wasn't her daughters fault. Jess had sent a note in as Sophie had been off sick and was advised to drink as much as possible. She had given the girl a bottle of water to take to school but, when Sophie had taken it out in class, the teacher, who had missed the memo, snatched it off of her and put it in the bin at the front of the class. Sophie had promptly gone to retrieve it and this had resulted in a tussle, during which Sophie managed to pull the teachers hair.

'NO. Mummy! why should I,' pointing a finger at the teacher, '*she* started it.'

The teacher looked just slightly embarrassed and decided to take the adult stand, despite looking about twelve. 'Sophie, I am sorry, I didn't know about the situation.'

Jess nudged her daughter. 'Go on.'

Sophie glared at her mother.

'Hair?' Jess responded.

Sophie looked at her feet and twisted one foot, lips pressed tightly together, then, very reluctantly, blurted out, 'Sorry 'bout your hair.'

The head let out the breath he had been holding in. 'Right, good, then we'll say no more about it then.' He stood to shake Jess by the hand, lingering slightly longer than necessary, and, as the group left his office, he retrieved the sandwich he had been halfway through on their arrival. She was certainly an attractive piece that mother, sensible too. Quite how the daughter was such a handful he couldn't understand. He shook his head as he dismissed the idea of asking her to dinner during the fast approaching summer break and took another bite of his lunch.

Jess got into her car in the school car park, unaware of the emotion she had stirred up. She put her head in her hands and was relived to realise there were only two more weeks of school, if Sophie could just stay out of the office till then. Maybe if she offered her a trip to Chessington in the holiday? If she made it towards the end she would have time to save up, even better, she may be able to hold it up as a sweetener through the start of the hols too? Oh, how she could be devious on occasion! she also knew Sophie didn't have to be at *school* to get into trouble. The doll incident, when Sophie had been four years old, had been one of the most memorable.

'Mrs Bartlett, it is *still* Mrs I suppose, only…' She left the rest unsaid.

Rude, she thought, but, unfortunately, correct.

'Now about this doll?' the smartly dressed woman on her doorstep held out her arms; doll in one hand, its right arm in the other. 'These are *very* expensive.'

Jess knew full well how much they cost, Sophie had wanted one for Christmas but, fortunately, they had sold out at the time as she wouldn't have been getting one any way, not at that exorbitant price! As with all these fad toys she had forgotten all about it by January. Until she went to play at Naomi's house. She wanted to play with the doll and Naomi had said no. Sophie picked it up anyway and the poor doll had come off worst. Now, it seemed so would Jess's pocket. This would cost at least two extra shifts.

'Obviously, I'll replace the doll, if you could give me a little time?' she watched the woman's face alter into a smug smile of satisfaction.

'Oh, I know you couldn't possibly afford to do that. But at least you have admitted it is your wayward child's fault. I don't want her playing with Naomi anymore.' Then she turned on her heel and strode off.

Sophie, who had overheard all of this, yelled down the stairs. 'Don't want to play with her anyway.' Then shut herself in her bedroom.

She was only four and already had a stubborn streak, Jess had sighed to herself, undecided whether to buy the new doll anyway or just forget the whole thing. A small glass of wine later she decided she just could not be bothered.

'Mummy? I'm hungry.' The plaintive voice of her adorable little girl was back. how could she be the devil and an angel at the same time.

'Do you want your favourite then?' Jess held out her arms and Sophie jumped on her lap as Jess hugged her, she had made a decision. She was not going to risk Sophie finding out from someone else that she wasn't her mother. They were moving.

'Your mother will be *fine* without you visiting as often, you've seen for yourself the condition of her. She doesn't remember what day it is, despite careful medication, her situation will not improve and, I daresay, will deteriorate over time.' The nurse smiled sympathetically at Jess.

'You still have your life to live and your mother wouldn't want it any other way. Especially with you taking on Sophie the way you have and as for Simon.' Mona left her opinion of him unsaid this time, probably because of the third party.

'What about you though?' Jess was concerned as Mona's children had both left now, her daughter for Uni and her son, having taken a liking for overseas, had not returned from his gap year jaunt. Jess also knew her uncle had been drinking more and more and Mona had even mentioned the 'D' word. Unheard of in their family, they had always believed in sticking by your own come what may and family was everything. That bit was still true, she knew. But times *had* changed.

Jess had not been as upset as she thought when she turned the key for the last time in the little cottage. Her mum's place had been snapped up by another young village couple, just starting out like her and Simon back when, and she couldn't help feeling a little jealous of them when she saw them come and go. When Louise had fallen pregnant and the new house new baby mantra was going around the terrace, again, she shut herself indoors for two days on the pretence of being ill! This was best all round. She was moving to the outskirts of a larger town, a countryfied suburb, it was a little further than the town nearest the village but she felt that she would still see too many old faces if she went there.

The new house was a rental and it was ideal till she found her feet, found a job and sorted a school for her little charge. The outside was pretty, with flint walls and a white painted front door. Wooden sash windows looked out over a courtyard garden, but there was a park nearby for Sophie to play in.
'Where is this going luv?' One of the guys asked her. It was a box of Simon's stuff.
'The nearest tip.' She replied, only half joking.
Simon's dad swooped in, 'I'll take that.' He had been great the last 18 months and Kate as well. They had stayed away for a while but they loved Jess like a daughter and, with all that had happened to Lucy and Dan, had been like surrogate parents. Still she wasn't sorry to be seeing less of them now. It was still a reminder, and, although they were careful not to mention Simon, some things inevitably slipped out.

'Bye, don't forget… anything you need, anything.' They both said together. Then hugged her and Sophie. Tears threatening to spill as they both thought of Sophie as the grandchild they hadn't had. They left with a wave and Jess shut the door.

'Can I play in my new bedroom Mummy?' Sophie looked up hopefully.

'After tea, poppet, after tea.' Jess busied herself making a sandwich and bought out the cake Mona had made for them, looked at it, picked a bit off and consigned it to the bin. Her cookery skills never had improved. She picked up the shop bought one that Kate had given her and unwrapped it, she boiled the kettle, laid the table and they sat together. Sophie's chatter filled the room and Jess was glad not to have to fill the silence. After tea Sophie could unpack her toys and…the silence outside was suddenly broken by an almighty banging and crashing coming from the back. Running into the small courtyard she could hear language and whining from over the wall. She peeked over and could just make out a pair of legs under a pile of wood, and caught sight of a dog disappearing into the back door. She realised the pile had been a shed until about two minutes ago.

'Are you okay?' She called.

'Does it look like it?' the wood pile started to move and a young man pushed his way up and out of the pile. 'OW, bloody OW.'

'Erm, my daughter…' Jess didn't want Sophie picking up that sort of language.

Sorry but,' he gestured his leg where blood was staining his torn jeans. Jess clambered over the wall and made him sit on the garden bench.

'Take off your trousers.'

'What, I, NO!'

Jess decided to lie a little. 'It's alright. I've seen it all before, I'm a nurse.' Oops, she could always say he'd misheard as he was in shock.

'Can you stitch it?' He asked after she had cleaned it with water and cotton-wool.

NO, she thought, she wasn't going *that* far. 'No, I can put butterflies on it.' It wasn't deep, just long. Seeing his puzzled expression she added. 'Little twists of plaster to hold it together.' She dressed it as he watched.

'So, Nurse?'

Jess brushed her hands and held one out. 'I'm Jess and my little assistant here is-,'

'I'm Sophie and I'm four.'

He raised an eyebrow and replied, 'Well, Sophie I'm four, my name is Justin.'

Sophie giggled, 'No, my name is just Sophie!' She squealed.

'It's a pleasure to meet you just Sophie.' He added, winking at Jess.

'Mummy, tell him!' She rounded on her mum.

The dog, that had sat in the corner watching warily joined them now and gently nudged at Sophie's arm.

'Barney,' Sophie grabbed the dog and cuddled it.

Jess looked alarmed. 'No, Sophie not all collies are Barney. And you should ask before touching.'

'He touched me first!' There was no answer to that really so Jess just smiled at Justin.

'He is a she, and she is the daftest dog you'll ever meet. And she LOVES children.' He looked at Jess who visibly relaxed but, unable to think of any more, said firmly,

'We must be off, unpacking and stuff.' Jess lifted the girl over the wall and Justin tried to stand. 'Stay there a bit, then rest it when you get inside.' She told him.

'Mummy can we get a dog?'

'NO. We can't.' She was a bit sharp and regretted it instantly.

Justin quickly called out. 'You can visit Molly anytime you like.'

Right, she'd met the neighbour and hoped his wife is as nice as him. She had seen a woman leaving earlier on and assumed, as she had been gone so long, she had gone to work.

It hadn't taken Jess long to find herself an office job at a small Estate Agents in the town. Sophie was in a school nearby so she could drop her off and pick her up on the way. The bus service was ideal for the journey. The job was working out fine. School? not so much. Sophie had had quite a lot of upheaval in her little life and once she had to leave Jess all day every day it became a bit much. She started acting up. When the tears didn't work, she started misbehaving in class, when that didn't work, she made out she was sick. This went on for weeks. At half term Jess sat her down and asked what exactly it was that made her like this, was she being bullied? NO. Was the teacher horrible? NO. Did she miss Jess? A bit. OK. But she had to work so she wouldn't see her anyway. Then she blurted out the meals were horrible, and they *made her* eat them, *and* she couldn't go to the toilet! And then she cried. After some cajoling and lots of cuddles it transpired that she had been told to eat her carrots one day and, when she said she needed to wee, the dinner lady took it upon herself to tell her she couldn't until she had finished. According to Sophie she was really scary and now she didn't want to go to school in case she wet herself! Jess went into the school to sort it out and sent a packed lunch instead. The rest of the term peace resumed.

The agents were very pleased with Jess and had started to send her out on viewings which she loved. Seeing all the ideas in other people's houses was like an addiction to her. she made up her mind to see about a design course.

One night in August she sat pouring over courses at the local college. There were so many that appealed to her. Floristry caught her eye several times as did interior design. As the floristry course was shorter, and therefore cheaper, she opted for that one. She had arranged with work that she could miss a day to attend the course as she had no one to look after Sophie. They were so pleased with her they had readily agreed. On the whole she thought, life was starting to come together. It had only been a few weeks but it felt like things were on the up. Not that she had time for that but she had even been asked on a few dates, which had at least restored some confidence in herself. And next door the brother and sister, not husband and wife as she first thought, were becoming good friends. They were there if needed they frequently told her. Lizzie had even offered to babysit if Jess had a date. She wasn't going to be taking her up on that one yet though. Justin had been brilliant too; when the washing machine had flooded the floor, the first time she switched it on, he came to rescue with tools and quickly rectified the loose fitting. Which would probably cost a fortune for a plumber, "they see a single woman and the price at least doubles." He'd joked and all it took was a quick tighten, fortunately the floor was tiled so it was quick and easy to clean up. Soon they were sharing a cup of tea and a sandwich at the kitchen table. The first of many.

'It's quite useful having the local handy man next door then.' Jess teased him one day when she came home to find him fixing her wonky gate. 'The least I can do is offer you and Lizzie some dinner. Especially with all those veg.' The pair grew a lot of vegetables and Jess often arrived home to find some fresh produce or other on the door step.

'That's nothing, wait till she gets going on the jam. I will expect a Victoria sponge at least, with the plum flavour.' He winked at her.

To her horror Jess felt the heat creep up her face. She laughed it off but inside? Was she starting to *like* him? She wasn't too sure about that idea. It was far too soon. Wasn't it? and she had Sophie to consider. No, best leave that sort of thing. She would have a word with Lizzie. Maybe.

Chapter Twenty-One

The sun was streaming down on the October morning two years later when she arrived at work and found, unbelievably, that her house was up for sale! She had got so used to being there and with her course and settling Sophie she had quite forgotten it was a rental.

'I'm afraid so.' Her boss looked sympathetic as he handed her back her paper work. 'You haven't signed for a set period he can do what he likes with it. He *should* have told you, but that wouldn't change anything. He wants the capital out of it so he won't renew anyway. You are just staying on a month to month basis. At least we should be able to find you something quickly from here.' He went on as if that made up for it.

'What's that Mummy?' Sophie asked as Jess worked on her college project.

'Sorry darling you need to be careful with that.' She extracted the pale cream flowers from the little girl. When Lizzie had heard about the floristry, she had helped Jess out with some flowers from their garden and, together with her own cottage garden, Jess's designs had been outstanding, according to her tutor who had even offered her a job at her own florists on Saturdays but Jess had to refuse. She had been kind enough to leave it open at, "anytime" when the course had ended. At least she had completed it before she had to leave here.

She sat looking around and wondered how she was going manage without Lizzie and Justin. She had become so used to them. It was like having a family back.

'You cannot be serious!' Lizzie did a great John McEnroe impression when Jess confided in her about the house. 'But, but it won't be the same without you! You're like the sister I never had.'

'What's all this then,' called a voice behind them as they hugged, both a little teary, 'and, what exactly is *wrong* with a brother might I ask?' He tried to sound put out, and failed.

Ever dramatic Lizzie replied, 'Jess and Sophie are being thrown out!'

Justin's face fell but he quickly recovered. 'They, but they, they can't just do that!'

Jess explained the situation as she served up the dinner that had become a regular Friday night ritual, albeit at six o'clock so everyone could get on with other things. This invariably meant Sophie going reluctantly to bed and Justin going to the pub where apparently most of his following weeks work was arranged. Lizzie sometimes went out with her boyfriend but, as he worked shifts, she would often keep Jess company for a couple of hours. 'So, I can't possibly afford to buy it. Believe me I have tried to work out every combination. The mortgage would be affordable, it's less than the rent! I even have extra work offers, at the Agency *and* the florist, but,' she shrugged and rubbed the little girl's hair. 'I just can't get a deposit. I have a little put by, but my other expenses cost a bit,' Jess let them think she meant Sophie. she hadn't told anyone here about her mum yet. Just saying she lived in her old village and left it at that. She mentioned the farm and her dad but that was as far as it went. Sophie was her daughter, she was divorced with an aunt who helped her. 'So, there it is.' She finished. The little group had cleaned their plates and Lizzie was putting Sophie to bed with a story. Jess was relieved as she had read her the same one all week now. Justin was helping her wash up, despite her insistence that she could manage and he should get along and find some work.

'Next week is pretty busy already.' He was nonchalant, but quieter than usual and when Lizzie was back down, he left anyway.

Chapter Twenty-Two

'OI!' Mel straightened up. 'Hands off.'

'Oh, c'mon luv, it *was* a target!' This from the slightly less drunk one of the four men sitting at the table Mel was trying to clear.

She grabbed their glasses and tried to stomp off, not an easy feat on the soft, white sand outside the beach bar. Inside she slammed the glasses down, Andy, behind the counter jumped and swung round, when he saw the thunder in her eyes and the frowny mouth he tried to make light of it.

'Bit frisky on the whisky, are they?' He smiled. She didn't.

'Think they can bloody well paw you, some of them. They,' she pointed out at the beach, 'are going to be trouble.'

'That's OK.' He looked at the few customers left. 'You might as well get off now. I can handle closing up here tonight.'

Mel threw down the towel she had been wiping the counter top with.

'Great. See you tomorrow then.'

Andy watched her leave. They had a great relationship. Now. He remembered the clumsy, drunken pass she had made toward him a couple of weeks after starting work. "You're just not like the other guys." She had whispered. She had got that right! Her usual guys, if this latest one was anything to go by, had huge muscles, sun tans, and, often, bad tempers. He was a small villager who worked farms and animals! Whilst giving her a listening ear and some advice she had taken it wrong and he had gently, but very firmly, explained that he was a mate, that was *definitely* all. The sound of shouts and breaking glass drew him back to the moment. Looks like Mel was right. He went outside to the four men seated at the table.

'Uh oh. Look busy here comes the boss.' One of them stage whispered bursting into hysterical fits.

Andy walked casually over, his attire of white long-sleeved tunic and baggy trousers essential to keep the sun off his skin, too much sunburn on the farm had taught him that one, was the source of yet more amusement.

'Ooh, look out the natives are *really* revolting.' Cried another one, as Andy reached the table.

'Donsh I no yooze' slurred the man who was slumped in a chair, one eye open as he grabbed Andy's sleeve.

Pulling his arm free, Andy quipped, 'I doubt you'd know your own mother at the minute.'

'Aww, for fucks sake Stu! You'd think you knew a bloody alien if it was in front of you after a pint. That accident really messed you up.' This bought forth many more laughs and some table drumrolls. The drunk slipped back down, as his eyes fell shut.

Andy decided the best course of action.

'Listen lads, it's time to close up now.'

'Thought you had twenty bloody four hour drinking over here mate.' One replied, then belched. It went on a long time.

'Different rules for beach bars.' This lie came in useful several times a year. 'But I can do you another round and you can stay there to enjoy them.' He smiled easily at the group, and held out his hands out in a non-threatening way.

'Cheers, same again then.' They threw some money on the table.

Andy picked it up adding rude, arrogant, pricks, to his image of them, and sauntered away with a, "whatever" gesture.

Inside he started to make the drinks to a chorus of nights, adios, manana, tomorrow bro. His clientele was certainly varied! They all seemed to end up here, like it was some last-ditch point, some before they went back home, some made this their home, and some, seeing the casual, laid back way of life, running as fast as they could back to civilisation. He, for one, was glad he had stumbled across it and had made the island his home for the past five years.

'Should he really be having any more?' Andy, placing the drinks on the table, feigned concern at the man slumped in the corner. If these tossers wanted to drink themselves dead then who was he to worry about it. He whistled as he walked off, grabbed the rubbish bag and a bottle of beer. He pulled the gates across the bar. They weren't a lot of protection but it was pretty crime free here. Just the odd drunken tourist trying their luck.

After leaving the village in 1996 his first stop abroad had been over in France. He had arrived at a small village and seen a sheep in distress in a field, after helping it he turned to see the farmer watching him. It transpired the farmer needed help, this was gleaned with the help of an English speaking local. The farmer first thought he looked too scrawny but when he saw him pick up the sheep he had been impressed. The experience gained on the farm back home had been really helpful and he had fitted in for a few months. When the man's son arrived home from college, he had a couple of close calls with him and decided to leave. Finding work on a nearby fruit farm he finished the summer there. He used up some of his savings heading for Paris where he worked in several bars and clubs for the winter. He heard about chalet work from some of the other staff and, after seeing in '97, he joined them to go to Switzerland and work the ski season. He found he was much in demand as a chalet staff. Even cooking the meals wasn't difficult. It wasn't to last though. On a drunken night one of the others had got a little too friendly with him and the bloody nose didn't go down too well with the management. Deciding he needed a bit of a change he went to the airport and took the first flight out. This was to Majorca and he spent a year here saving and learning. His love of islands was born. There was something entirely different about living on island. People here just seemed to take you at face value, no matter how strange you might be, it was normal. The wandering was inbuilt now though and one year on he was hankering for a change, in more ways than one.

He settled back into the seat and closed his eyes. Only to be rudely shoved awake by someone trying to get in the seat next to him.

'Sorry is usual.' His sarcasm was lost on the girl.

'Hi, I'm Mattie.' The deep voice was a shock.

It must have shown, as she carried on. 'Short for Matilda. I'm waiting for a voice op. or maybe some vocal training?' She smiled, as if this was the most natural thing in the world.

Andy stared at her face, closer, at the slight roughness around it. He put out his hand.

'It's a *real* pleasure to meet you.' Andy smiled back. On that journey, he learnt a *lot*. And now he knew. He was going to Germany.

A painful and enlightening year later he entered Amsterdam and found lodgings in a cheap hotel, no questions asked, cash only. They did insist on strict rules so the place was actually pretty quiet. It suited him as a place to rest, recuperate, heal his wounds and make some decisions. After he had been there for a couple of weeks, he walked in one day as the current manger was getting sacked. He had let one of the rooms to his own sister, for free!

'Oi, you, do you have family here?'

He walked on without realising he was being spoken to.

'Hey, you, Red.'

He turned at that. 'No, I guess not.'

'Great.' The man then threw the keys at him. 'Have a job. Free lodgings. Don't be a wanker. I can tell you need a job. Take it.'

Catching them, he looked at them for just a minute then walked behind the counter and picked up the ringing phone. The pay was pretty rubbish but it meant he didn't dip into his savings and the work was light. A few years here with no questions or odd looks and a chance to recoup his savings. Things were good. He did miss the family sometimes though but he knew they didn't understand him. Nothing out of the ordinary for them.

Andy was back at the bar early the next morning. It had been hot and sleep had alluded him. As he approached along the white sand, he could see one of his brollies was lying in the water. Bloody drunks must've been messing about last night. As he got closer, he could see it wasn't a shade but a man. He was laying with his head in the water, no shirt and only one sandal on, the other was floating in on the tide a bit further along. Andy knew exactly who it was. He looked up the beach to the tables where the men had been sitting. He could see two more of them, one across the table, his head nearly touching the sand and one on his side on the sand with a chair cushion under his head. His attention went back to the man at his feet and he nudged him over with his foot. It was too late. The man was, most definitely, dead. Andy couldn't help a rueful smile, whistling he carried on over to the table, picked up all the empty glasses then went around the front to open the bar. He opened the bar door and loudly put the glasses on the bar, breaking one in the process. The two men stirred and he called out, 'good night then lads?' He pointed towards the body, 'but swimming on a pissed stomach is never a good idea.' one of them gave a shout of alarm, Andy turned to see him running towards his mate at the waters edge. He went back behind the bar and switched on the glass washer, went out to the public bin to put the wrapped, broken one away then, on his return, as the man called for help, he finally picked up the phone. Paradise lost.

He watched the police activity, the cars arriving and leaving, dropping off more workers, the busy scene such a contrast to the normal landscape. He made a decision. Mel walked in the bar and he threw the keys at her and left, feigning illness, packed quickly, and was on the next flight off the island. Maybe it was time to try and make contact. He'd been watching Jess's face-book for some time now and couldn't believe all that had happened and how much Sophie had grown. Perhaps he should reach out now. Scared, that's what he was, it had been so long, family was family that's what they always said but after this amount of time? He wanted to stay away before but now? He didn't want to admit it but he was lonely. He was sort of used to it but, if there was a chance? Maybe soon. A holiday. That's what he needed. Many would say he had been on one for years. He hadn't, it had been bloody hard work. A month off. He needed time to think.

Chapter Twenty-Three

'Just going for lunch Jess. Hold the fort.' Mr Attlee dashed past.

'No problem.' She grabbed the ringing phone as he left. A voice she knew only too well asked for her. 'Speaking.' She replied, a knot in her stomach. 'Not again! Can't it wait…I see. OK. Fifteen minutes then.' Jess reluctantly put the closed sign on the door with a note to say open at 2pm. As she got into her car her boss tapped on the window.

'Going somewhere?' he asked, the impatience not so well hidden.

'School, I …it's-,'

'I gathered. Keys please.' He held out his hand.

Jess rummaged in her back and handed them to him all the while trying not to throw them. 'I shan't be long.' She looked at him apologetically. Did it really require him to sack her?

'Hmm.' Was all he answered as he walked away.

Jess and the deputy head stood looking at Sophie and a scruffy boy, quite a bit bigger than her daughter, in a torn uniform.

'He started it.' Sophie pointed at the boy, 'he called me a ba-,' she looked at the adults. 'said my mother is a tart as I have no dad. But I do. I do have a dad, don't I Mum?'

'Sophie this fighting it is not the answer.' The head tactfully ignored the reasoning.

'Of course, I will pay for the shirt.' Jess rummaged for her purse as the head held up a hand.

'That won't be necessary, we have plenty in lost property.' In a better condition than this one was left unsaid. 'Run along to lost property Ryan and we will say no more about the language.' The boy started to open his mouth but one look from the head and he realised he was also on thin ice.

Jess looked at Sophie, her arms were crossed and a defiant look was fixed on her face. The long dark curls hung down over her shoulders and Jess was reminded, once again, of her lost sister. She sighed deeply. She grovelled some thanks to the headmaster, told Sophie she would deal with her later and went back to the Agents to collect her things and maybe grovel a bit for her job.

'Ah, you're back. Good. I have a viewing,' he looked at his watch, 'ten minutes ago.'

Ouch, another dig. 'Sorry I'll just get my things,' he would be in no good mood now he was rushing out the again.

'Back in half an hour.' He continued, 'and could you phone the Tenbeys? they had a viewing and I need to know how it went.'

'But the keys…? You took them back. I thought…' Jess stammered, unsure of herself.

'What? oh, yes,' he saw her puzzled and worried face. 'I didn't have mine with me. You didn't think...Oh Jess. Don't be silly.' He was gone before he even saw the relief on her face. She sat at her desk with her head in her hands, thankful she still had her job as she loved it here, and wondered if parenting was really meant to be this hard. For the first time in ages she wished she had her own mum to turn to. Aunt Mona was great, especially since her son, then her husband, had taken off. She still found it hard to imagine Uncle Phil floating around on a boat, like a water hippy. She giggled at that and, suitably cheered, she went to make a cup of very strong coffee.

Jess hadn't seen her neighbours all week and when Thursday came and went, with no sign of either of them, Jess assumed that, despite their previous closeness, they had moved on expecting her to leave any second. Her sadness was compounded when she arrived home to see a sold board outside. She couldn't help it, she burst into tears.

'I didn't think we were that bad as neighbours go.' A male voice behind her asked. She turned and saw Lizzie and Justin. Both had the biggest smiles on their faces.

'What's going on?' Jess looked blankly from one to the other.

'Do you think I'll make a bad landlord Lizzie?' Justin looked sideways at his sister.

'Sorry, sorry, sorry, we have been so distant this week, but I didn't want to blurt out something before we were sure. And I *would* have.' Lizzie squeaked.

'She would.' Justin grinned at his sister. Knowing full well she couldn't have kept quiet he had literally banned her from talking to Jess.

'What are you talking about?' Jess asked as she wiped her face in her hands.

He walked across and pulled out the sold board, while Lizzie started nodding frantically at her.

Jess, understanding starting to dawn, looked from one to the other. 'But…how?' then burst into tears again, happy ones. Sophie, not understanding, promptly burst out crying too.

Since Jess and Sophie had been given a definite roof over their heads and, with school and work settled, Jess had time to think about her mum. She missed her *so* much. The accident had been such a big shock. The brain damage it had left her with had been stabilized for several years now but the Mum she knew was gone, despite being here physically. She sat at the table stripping leaves from the stems of the flowers she was arranging into posies, for the bride to collect later that morning. On a chair in the corner sat a beautiful white and peach arrangement for the bride herself. This bought her sentimental feelings of her own wedding but she stood up, poured some water in a glass, sipped it slowly, and the cold liquid soon settled her. What was she going to do about her mum? The best option, she knew, was to leave her where she was. The feeling of letting her down was still big inside her. it was alright for the doctors to say she was better off there but she was her *mum*. Shouldn't she be looking after her. Sophie chose that moment to come running in and, looking at her Jess realised that this *was* helping. Taking on Sophie had been the best thing she could have done. It would have been so easy to let Mona take her, and would have probably saved her marriage too. Maybe not. She would have wanted children at some point and Simon was still a long way from being that grown up.

'Mummy, Mummy look what Molly can do. I just taught her!'

The dog sat behind Sophie and she turned around to her.

'Molly, roll over.' As she said it she turned her arm in a circle. Justin appeared over the fence with his fingers to his lips. Jess had seen him teach her this trick earlier in the week.

'Well done you!' Jess smiled at her and ruffled the black curls.

'Mummy could I have my hair cut? For my birthday?' Sophie asked.

'Why? You have beautiful hair!' Jess was dismayed.

'I just…I want to?

Jess knew something had bought this on, but what? there had been no trouble at school for ages and she knew that Lizzie always said she wished she had Sophie's hair. So, it wasn't a question of copying her new idol.

'Sophie, what is it?'

'I want to give some to Lizzie, she has only got thin straggly hair and she loves mine.'

Jess Laughed out loud at this. 'Oh Sophie, Lizzie doesn't want *your* hair! She just wishes her hair was so curly and thick. You are lucky you know you got your…grandad's hair not something like my straight stuff! Jess had had her own hair cut a few months back, the longer length inverted bob really suited her. She looked smart, modern and sassy. When she had seen herself in a mirror, wearing a suit for work and her new soft make-up and hair she could not believe the confident looking woman looking back was her!

'WOW. Lizzie had said when she showed herself. What did you do with my friend and why are you wearing her shoes! Seriously, you look amazing.'

'I feel a bit...' Jess pulled a face and waved her hands up and down her length to show she felt self-conscious.

Lizzie grabbed an arm and tucked it through Jess's. In an over the top, haughty voice she replied. 'Oh, *dharling*! Fake it 'till you make it!'

Jess gripped her hand and realised again how lucky she was to have found Lizzie. And Justin. It had been 18 months since they had bought her house and he had realised that Jess had Sophie and her mum to focus on, but let it be known that he was here whenever or whatever she needed or wanted. She was grateful for that but knew deep down he wouldn't wait forever. But she still had time. Plenty of time. She took him a cup of tea out to the garden and they watched as Sophie repeated the new trick. Over and over and over.

'How come you never mention Sophie's dad? Justin asked later when Sophie had finally given up teaching Molly and gone off to watch the TV. 'I mean I know she sees his parents but you,' he saw her face and quickly backtracked, 'sorry, I just, anyway, Sophie's looking forward to her next trick.' Jess relaxed and harmony was restored. She hated that she was lying, well, misleading them both over her situation but she had been this way for so long she couldn't see any way out.

Chapter Twenty-Four

'I *really* am pleased you got back in touch you know. It's just that…with Mum…' she tailed off.

'I know you miss your sister, it was harder on you, being a twin, I *do* realise that but you gained a daughter.'

Jess had a quick flash of the lows and then the highs of motherhood and had to agree.

'And you still have me, we are still family.'

'How is Uncle Phil? I gather you ran into him?'

'Yeah…he's a bit off his tree these days though. Thinks he's an artist cos he painted some crappy flowers on the side of his boat! *Piss* artist is more like.'

'Language!'

'Oh, come on! He is a waste of space.'

'Be nice! Sophie already thinks we are all a bit odd. No one else she knows talks to relatives abroad. And most families grow, ours is going backwards!'

Chapter Twenty-Five

'Happy birthday to you, happy birthday to you.' Sophie and Lizzie came in with a cake with 30 candles on it.

'You really need to blow these out quickly or they will set fire to the cake in a minute! Sophie spilled the rum flavouring.' Lizzie laughed.

'Yeah, you could get pissed on that cake Mum!' Sophie joined in.

'Sophie!' Since returning to school after Christmas her daughter had been mixing with a rough crowd, her language wasn't the only appalling habit she had picked up. She had been caught smoking, truanting and even, on one occasion, bullying. She had morphed, overnight, into an alien. Just as suddenly she could be the sweetest little thing on the planet. Teenagers, apparently. Everyone told her this was normal. It would pass. Jess hoped so.

That evening she was looking at her Facebook page. She was still amazed how much business she could get from this and had to check it every day now. She didn't take every job that came along as she still liked working at the estate agent and she never took on funeral work, far too depressing, but the flowers were certainly a useful income. Last week she had made enough to cover Sophie's new school uniform.

'MUUM, Uncle Andy wants a word with you.' Sophie followed her voice into the kitchen 'He's on skype.'

'Just coming, but aren't you going to say goodbye?' Jess watched Sophie pull a face and shrug her shoulders.

'You can tell him.' With that, she shot up the stairs followed by the sound of the bedroom door as she slammed it shut. Jess knew she would have to talk to her later.

'Hi Jess.' Andy's face filled the screen. The suntan obvious and the wet hair glinted with chestnut hues as he sat on his veranda, mountains in the background.

'Hi, how you doin'?'

'Yeah, yeah, good. Just called to wish us a happy birthday. Also, to remind you that I am younger than you. Ha.' He sighed. 'God, Jess. She is *so* grown up. You've done such a good job, I,' He broke off.

'Don't. I just did what anyone would have done.' Jess brushed off the compliment. 'Did you hear about Stuart Hodder? He died, drowned they think. Quite a while back somewhere abroad. Mona heard about it in the local shop. It was a bit thirty-third hand, as his family moved away after the hit and run. Isn't that the same person involved with the accident?' They both knew she was referring to the hit and run with Lucy.

'Yes. He wasn't so lucky after all, was he?'

Jess took a sharp breath. 'Neither was Mum.' They both went quiet for a second, each lost in thought. After that they said their goodbye's and Jess headed towards the stairs.

'Sophie.' No response. 'Sophie. Come down here. Now please.' She heard the door open and returned to the kitchen to make the tea.

'Right. what is up with you?' She gave Sophie a, "don't bother pretending" face and Sophie started to speak.

'It. It's, um, Andy.'

'What about him?' Jess was genuinely puzzled.

'He…says stuff.' Sophie looked at her feet.

Jess went to laugh then thought better of it. 'What stuff? What do you mean Sophie?'

'Stuff. Y' know? He's always saying I'm pretty, or aren't I getting grown up, and he gets this…weird look on his face.'

'Well,' said Jess, relieved that this was all. 'You are pretty and you are growing up!'

Sophie dropped her shoulders. 'But it's, creepy. And he's not even a *real* uncle. I know. You told me when I was younger.'

'Oh Sophie. No. That's true. But he is close family. And I don't have much of that left now. When we were on the farm all the family were around but with all the losses.' She broke off, took a breath and continued. 'I was really pleased when Andy contacted me. Us.' She corrected quickly.

'Is there something you aren't telling me?' Sophie stared at her mum. 'Oh. God. He's not my *real* father, is he? Was it something like that? Mum. He isn't, is he?' Sophie was getting quite excited now, her eyes were large and glowing.

'NO.' Jess spluttered, 'No Sophie. Andy is *definitely* not your father.' She started to laugh then.

'Then he is plain old weird.' Sophie sank back into the chair.

He is not weird.' Her defence was automatic. 'He is just a little…different.'

'That's what you say about Grandma. Are all our family just bloody odd?'

Jess bit her lip. 'All families are different, in their own way.' She shrugged, wanting to drop the subject. 'So, what do you want for tea, anyway.'

Sophie, realising the conversation was closed, blew out her lips. 'Whatever.'

Chapter Twenty-Six

'I am sorry. I have to go. It's Sophie.' He gave her the, "again" look and waved a hand at her. She was his best employee and having met Sophie, and having teenagers of his own, albeit boys, he knew it was just a phase. It was turning out to be quite a bloody long one though.

'Ms Collier your daughter has been caught shoplifting. It is quite a serious matter.' The store manager stared at her hard. 'We have far too much of this at the moment *and,* they *should* be in school.' He looked at the three girls in front of him. Jess was the only parent to have rushed in and the other two sat chewing gum and joking about. Only Sophie had the decency to look shamefaced and peered intently at something, non-existent, on the floor. He walked to the door with the pair of them and added. 'You may be hearing from the police shortly.' Once outside he pulled her aside from Sophie and spoke directly and even kindly to her. 'Look, I know you, you sold me my house, last year?' Jess reddened. 'It's fine, really I won't press charges against your daughter but the other two? This is the third time now and I really have to do something. I *will* have to ban Sophie, for now, but please, get her to stay away from those two, they are really bad news.'

'We can change school but you can't go to Uni Sophie unless you knuckle down now and get your exams. I will even pay for extra tuition and you can re-sit but you have to really want it.' Jess crossed her fingers that she would somehow find the money for that one. Sophie had been in trouble yet again, this time it was for bullying. She had promised her that she would stay away from the girls. It wasn't really Sophie, it was the girls she was hanging with but she was tarred. She couldn't believe it at first but the bullies were the same ones who had picked on Sophie and it was a case of join or be damned. 'It is *your* future you are throwing away. When you go to sixth form *you* have to make the effort, they won't force you, just throw you out.' Jess looked exasperated at her 15 going on 23yr old daughter. 'It's your call.'

Fortunately, Sophie settled into sixth form and put her old habits behind her, the bad crowd had left and she had soon settled and made new friends. Nice ones, Jess imparted to her employer. After another year Jess finally relaxed. Just in time for the search for a University.

'Mrs Bartlett,' they still referred to her back there under her married name, 'could we have a quick word please?' The manager of the home popped her head round the door.
'Of course, back in a minute Mum.' Jess smiled at her mum and stood up, not noticing her phone slip out of her pocket and onto the chair she had just vacated.

Lucy stared at the picture on the screen. Dropping the phone had bought it to life and a photo of Sophie appeared on the screen with a group of youths and, in the centre, an older dark haired man. He seemed familiar. Her brain couldn't quite connect the dots. It would come to her she was sure. Usually in the middle of a dream. Or rather the drug induced, fuddled state of her sleep.

'Mum? I'm sorry but I have to go now.' Jess knew the visit had been a bit short but she had *so* much to do, sorting out Sophie for Uni. She saw the phone in Lucy's hand and saw the picture she was looking at.

'Oh, that's Sophie with some of the student hopefuls at the Uni. She met on an intro day last week. They looked a nice group.' Jess smiled at her mum as she took back the phone and kissed her, quickly, on her forehead. 'Love you.' And she was gone.

Lucy sat in her chair, watching out the window at the birds, trees and fields outside. She fell asleep. Something stirred in her. Inside her muddled, foggy brain. A girl? A child? Her Daughter. Another daughter. Not Jess? It was so fuzzy…it was HIM. She sat bolt upright in her chair. The photo it *was* him. Was he? Had he?... He had! Somehow, she just knew he had… attacked her little girl. The same way he had her, all those years ago…

'You know I really like you Lucy? Don't you. It's not like you don't like me, is it. It'll be okay. I promise.'

The teenage girl looked at the older boy with his arm round her. He smiled reassuringly and started to peel off her school cardigan. When she pulled away he got firmer. 'Now then Lucy, you can't pretend you don't want it too.' Then he kissed her, hard, and pushed her back to the ground.

After that she avoided him. At least avoided being alone with him. He was leaving school soon anyway. Then he would be gone. For good.

He turned back up, ten years later, to live in his old family home when his parents had passed away, bringing a wife and a little boy the same age as her twins. He barely acknowledged her in the street. By then she had settled with Dan. When they had first made love she had been apprehensive, but if he had noticed he never said. In his arms she felt safe, warm and loved.

'Dinner, Lucy. You can have it in your room today as we have had a bit of a problem in the dining room.' A pipe had burst and all hands were involved in the clearing up process.

Lucy stared at the girl wishing she would just go away. The tray was placed in front of her and she sat. Holding the knife. Stabbing at the soft piece of roast chicken on the cold, white, china plate. Clink, clink, clink…

'What do mean? Missing! How can she be bloody missing? You are a secure facility. At least I thought you were.' Jess, in traffic on her way to the florist for supplies, found panic setting in. She pulled over. 'I'll be right there.' She sent a quick text to Sophie and spun the car around to head towards the home.

'We are not a *secure* facility we have no padlocks! Just the number locks. It appears she went out of her window. The staff were very busy,'

'BUSY? What mopping the bloody floor!' Jess was exasperated at the woman's explanation.

'The staff are carrying out a thorough search…yes?' She turned as her assistant came in. She shook her head. 'OK. Perhaps the police?' She turned to Jess.

'About time!'

'It has only been an hour Mrs Bartlett.' The manager said gently. 'Tea.' To her assistant.

The police arrived in fifteen minutes and soon had a search underway. It was getting dark though so they had bought a dog and torches. Getting organised took another fifteen minutes and Jess was climbing the walls.

'Wait here Jess.' The policeman said to her as she tried to join them.

She paced the corridor for what seemed like hours. She spoke to Sophie. No, no news. She had gone around to next door and they sent their best and fed Sophie. She was so grateful for them.

Jess sat nodding her head as she tried not to fall asleep in a chair when, at 1.30, a pathetic, wet, muddy Lucy was bought through the front door. Her nightie was torn and filthy, one foot held a muddy slipper the other was bare, scratched and bloody. So were her bare arms, one of which had quite a gash. Barbed wire. The policeman suggested. The police dog had found her, curled up asleep under a kid's camp shelter in the woods.

The staff whisked her away for a bath and a warm up. They threw her torn, filthy clothes in the bin. It was yellow bag collection tomorrow and the waste was due to be taken for incineration. She was washed, warmed then put to bed with sleeping pills. She was quite distraught and mumbling about protecting, or not protecting, your young. She was still asleep next morning when the talk of the village was the suspicious death of Mr Allenby, a quiet man who lived in the old Emsworth house. He had been stabbed, just once, in the neck. His ex-wife was being sought. It seemed her maintenance payments had just finished as their youngest child having just finished school. She swore they had not argued but the timing of the phone call she made to him was incriminating. And, he had been heard to scream by a local, out walking their dog. It was just the once and they had assumed it must have been an animal. Also, unfortunately, she had no alibi.

Chapter Twenty-Seven

'Hi, I'm Serena. I think were sharing?' the dark-haired chubby girl held out a hand to Sophie's back then put it, self-consciously, back in her coat pocket. 'Yeah, um, well… I'm doing Sociology what about you?' She continued.

'Yeah, I'll be there in five.' Sophie spun round and fell over the new girls' suitcase. 'Who the hell are you?'

'I'm, like, um Serena?' Then she saw the head phones Sophie was removing from her ears and realised she hadn't heard a word.

'Hello, like Serena, I am definitely Sophie. Dump your stuff and come on.'

The girl looked puzzled.

'Student bar? Sociable?'

'Um, I.'

Sophie flicked a hand. 'Whatever.' And left the girl staring after her.

'Yeah, yeah I got the short straw I guess, "Um, I…Um". Sophie was deep into the impression of the girl who was now, typically, standing right behind her. 'Well, if isn't like Serena.'

'Um, my name is just Serena?' The girl replied in confusion.

'Sit.' Sophie made everyone shuffle up, 'C'mon, sit, sit.' She patted the chair next to her. The girl put her drink down and spent the next few minutes being introduced to everyone. Twice. First their real names, then their nicknames. She was totally overwhelmed and Sophie saw she was going to either have to take her under her wing or else leave her out of everything and sharing a room could make both options awkward. She chose the first one.

'Ooh. Are you seeing him again?' Sophie took in the red wrap round top and the short black skirt, black opaque tights and to complete the outfit…clumpy, black lace-up shoes. 'Oh what! I know we are students and a bit broke but *really*? Those?!'

Serena looked at her shoes, 'What's wrong? I always wear these. They're comfy.'

Sophie threw her a look that said, "exactly", and went to rummage in her wardrobe, she pulled out some heeled, black sandals and threw them at her friend. 'Much better' she looked at the girl in the mirror.

Serena pulled a face. 'I'm not sure, they aren't really me, shouldn't he like me as I am?'

'Of course, but sometimes you have to make a *little* effort. You don't want him going off with that American, do you?' Sophie had seen how upset Serena had been when Sadi had been pushing her chest in Paul's face over the desk.

'No!'

'Well then, give him something to look at, your legs are great.' Sophie turned back to the mirror and continued to line her eyes, blot her lips and kiss herself in the mirror.

'Who's all *your* effort for then?' Serena looked at Sophie who carefully avoided eye contact by checking for an imaginary hair across her face.

'No one special.' She shrugged.

'Is this the same "no one special" as the last three times?' Serena's eyes sparkled.

'Mm. Maybe. Don't wait up.' Sophie grabbed her bag and shot out the door before Serena could ask her any more questions. Her head came back through the door, 'Have a great time. Catch up tomorrow. Wine on me.'

Sophie stood in the shadows outside the dorms and saw Serena leave with Paul. Even at that distance she could see he was looking down at her with an appreciative look on his face and, when Sadi walked by and tried to attract his attention, he just walked on by with his arm laid casually around Serena's shoulders. Sophie found him a little…strange, probably unfair, he was just a bit quiet, but then Serena was quite a studious, serious girl so they were probably suited. A low whistle behind her caused her to start and, as the hand came around her neck, she quickly turned…and smiled as he ran a hand up her back.

'Hi.'

'Hi yourself.' He kissed her ear, then her neck.

'Hey, not so fast.'

'Aw, looking like that how could I not?'

Sophie whacked his arm and dragged him off. 'We'll be late. It starts in fifteen minutes.'

'Later then?' He threw her puppy dog eyes, going for hopeful and cute. He didn't quite achieve it.

'Mm. Maybe.' She teased him and they walked off out of the brightly lit entrance towards the cinema.

'That was brill.'
'Best film I've seen.'
'That bit about-,'' The voices at first all as one drifted apart as the entrance spewed out the crowd.
'How about a beer?' Sophie headed towards the student bar.
'I thought maybe some alone time?' He replied as he gripped her hand.
'Hey, what's all that?' The blue lights lit up the garden area ahead of them as they turned the corner. A stretcher was wheeled across in front of her.
'Serena?' Sophie choked as her friend was taken past. 'I don't understand she was going out with Paul tonight. What happened?'
'Miss?' a tug on her sleeve caused her to look up at the officer. 'Did you say you know who she was with?'
Startled, Sophie blurted out Paul's full name and where to find him. The officer spoke into his radio and the security guard appeared and led the man away to where the young student lived. A few minutes later he was bought out in handcuffs, shouting and kicking in a way Sophie had never seen him before. The door closed on the back of the ambulance and, before they could shut the second one, Sophie dove for it and yelled, 'I'm coming with her.' The door slammed. leaving Thomaz to stand alone in the driveway. He kicked the nearest post and headed off for a beer.

'She's my friend.' Sophie was protesting as Thomaz asked her out yet again. Secretly she was pleased to have the excuse. Serena had been scared to go anywhere by herself and Sophie had taken it on herself to be her personal guardian. There had been no evidence linking Paul to the attack and even Serena was sure it hadn't been him,

'He felt…bigger. Paul is very slight. this man felt more…solid.' Serena had told the officer at the hospital. Luckily whoever it was had been scared off before he could do any worse. But mud sticks and the boy had been bullied, shunned, and more; eventually he left for another university. The real culprit was never found and the girls had taken to going about in pairs for a few weeks; it didn't last. Everything went back to normal. Except for Serena. Sophie came in one day to find a note with no forwarding address and a thank you for being a good friend. Serena said she felt if they stayed in touch she would always be reminded of her attack.

Sophie was hurt and upset as one of her tutors found her crying in the garden. He offered her a tissue followed by a hug. 'Don't tell anyone. They'll all want one.' He joked with her. 'That's better, nearly a smile, I did want to see you actually.' The puzzled look she gave him caused him to quickly continue. 'About your course work. But it can wait.' He smiled back at her and it lit up his eyes and creased the corners of his mouth.

'No. no I'm fine. Thank you, for…' she held up the tissue.

'Hey, no probs. What are friends for?' He held up his hands and added, 'cool?'

'It's fine, what did you want to see me about?'

'Let's go to my office. I'll even make the coffee.' He knew better than to ask what it had been about.

Sophie looked at her watch.

'Somewhere to be?' The smile didn't quite reach his eyes this time.

'No. just need to ring my mum, later's fine.' She replied.

'Make yourself comfy.' He fiddled about with the coffee machine as Sophie flopped down on the battered black leather sofa.

She looked around the walls at the various pictures and certificates. 'Is that your girlfriend?' She asked seeing a picture of a much younger version of him with his arms round a pretty girl.

'What, no that's my sister! We were at our parent's anniversary party.'

'You must be close.'

'Not so much now. Here you go. Sugar?'

'Honey.' Sophie's joke, although old seemed to pass him by. 'What did you want to talk about?'

'Well,' He put his coffee on the table and joined her on the sofa. 'I like to get to know my students, especially the bright ones.' He smiled at her. 'What you want to do later, your ambitions. Is there a particular area of law you might want to practice? Do you want to just make lots of money, have an easy time, help people? What are *your* priorities?'

'Wow.'

'I know it's a lot to take in but you have to think about these things. I can tailor you some extra work, take into account your choices as we go along. That way when you finally leave, not too soon you are mine for the next five years,' a cheeky grin, 'you will be in a better position. You will know where you are going and you will have already some experience in your preferred area. Get you a head start out in that scary big wide world.' He widened his eyes, pulled a face and wiggled his hands. 'Don't you think?'

Sophie laughed at the scary face. 'It certainly never entered my head that there would be so many options. I *will* have to give it some thought.' She placed her cup on the table, gathered her bag and stood to go.

'My door is always open Sophie.' He shook her hand and held it…a little too long.

She pulled it away, and looked at his face, she took in the slightly too long, dark, wavy hair, then into his eyes. Nope, no leering, lecherous look, like she had from Thomaz just a kind teacher. She made her way out the door.

'For you.' He added, not quite loud enough for her to hear.

Sophie sat with the foils in her hair that contained the bright, red highlights she had been assured would complement her dark curls. She bloody hoped she was right, tonight was important. She enjoyed coming here. The student hairdressers in the college next door were always so relaxed and fun. Trisha had been doing Sophie's hair for the last couple of months and she was really chatty, always full of the night before and drunken tales of her friends falling down or naked swimming in the sea at midnight. Sophie envied her a little. She would have had so much fun with this lot but she had been doing so well with her studies and it was her choice, as her very proud mum *kept* pointing out. She rolled her eyes at the memory of her end of year reports. Hers had been absolutely glowing. She had had a LOT of extra work though, and tutorials late into the night, she giggled.

'It wasn't funny!' The stylist had been talking about her friend going to A and E.

'No. sorry, just reminded me of something.' She felt in her pocket for a sweet and found the crisp notes that Andy had sent her. "For doing so well, all my love." *and* a couple of kisses. She shuddered. Still creepy.

'Ooh thanks, wine gums my faves.' Trisha popped it in and kept quiet, for all of thirty seconds. 'So why don't you?'

'Sorry, what?'

'Why don't you come with us, tonight, to the pub?'

Sophie thought of her plans for later. 'Sorry, no can do.' She pulled a very bad American drawl to take the edge off the rebuttal.

The hairdresser still took offence. 'Hmm, not good enough for you *loyeerrs*.' She sniffed then pulled out one of the foils.

'Hey! That hurt aren't you supposed to *unwrap* them first.'

The girl sauntered off as she called, 'they can come off now,' to the bored looking first year student.

In town that afternoon Sophie walked by the expensive looking boutique, then stopped. Through the window, in the corner of the shop, she caught sight of every students' favourite word. SALE. She knew it would probably still be expensive but it couldn't hurt to look. Could it?

'Hi, are you looking for something…special?' the girl asked her, after she had watched her rummage for about ten minutes.

'Date. Tonight. Bit too expensive for a student though.'

The girl took pity on her. 'You know, I think there is just the thing out the back for you. Wait there.' She came back with a velvet and satin black dress and held it up to Sophie. 'Try it on.'

Sophie came out of the changing room a few minutes later and the girl came and over, turned Sophie to the mirror and held up her hair, letting tendrils fall round her face. The red highlights gave her hair a beautiful glow and they both stared at the vision in the glass.

'Amazing! Is that really me?'

'I thought it would suit you.'

'But how much is it?'

'I'll do you a deal. This is my shop.'

God, thought Sophie she didn't look old enough.

Alexandra read her mind. 'It was my Aunts, she's ill.' She shrugged and went on, 'and it needs new blood. Despite Aunt Corrine having impeccable taste. So, I've arranged a fashion evening. I need models. You're perfect. Favour for a favour?' she looked hopeful.

In response Sophie grinned at the reflections in the mirror.

At home Sophie pulled open her wardrobe doors to gain access to the mirror. Tonight, she thought, tonight it *will* be tonight. He was taking her to the Italian restaurant in the nearby town. Shouldn't be anyone there they knew, "no one could afford it" he joked. She had spent Andy's money on some new make-up and a pair of exceptionally high heeled nude court shoes. Just like the ones the royals wear the sales girl had said. She sat in front of the mirror, smoothing on the new foundation, it was as light as air. Next, she picked up the tongs and with the help of some You-tube videos she pulled, curled and pinned her hair. She didn't recognise the girl who looked back. She took the dress from the door, carefully removed the hanger and slid it on, the shoes next. A last look at the reflection before quietly closing her door, tiptoeing down the stairs and out the front door before anyone could see her or question her. Tonight, was hers, and hers alone.

'Steady there.' Mike opened the door of the restaurant for Sophie as they left and put his arm around her shoulders as he walked her across the carpark. At the car he held, the now rather tipsy, Sophie a bit tighter as she stumbled into the car. 'Did I tell you how wonderfully stunning you look, by the way.'
'Only about fifty-seven times.' Sophie said, slipping off her shoes in the footwell.

'Let's make it fifty-eight, then shall we?' When he had seen her walk towards his car earlier, he had had to do a double take. She was unrecognisable, unbelievable from the girl he had taken under his wing, some would say groomed, a year ago now. It had been a slow progress but looking at her tonight it had most definitely been worth it. He had topped up her glass at every chance, charmed and entertained her all evening and over coffee he had even thought that this one maybe, just maybe, a keeper. Or at least fairly long term. He could not *wait* to start removing that dress. He counted his blessings that he had managed to keep this position, it had *so* many perks! The only hiccup in the evening had been when she had mentioned the modelling. No fucking way was anyone else getting to see a piece of *his* property. But that was for another day… Tonight, she was his…and his alone.

Chapter Twenty-Eight

'I am sorry, but that's the way it is. You messed up. It may only be a small thing but it is enough to get you struck off. You must have known it was a possibility.' This was said as statement not a question. The man behind the desk stood, dismissively.

Mike stood up to leave and spoke in a whiny voice to the man in front of him. 'But, what do I do now?'

I don't bloody know, it was your mistake, live with it.' Then, as he remembered he was the son of a close friend he relented, a little. 'Go teach? A small college or Uni, maybe. Somewhere your past won't catch up with you.' A slight pause before he added, 'any of it.'

Mike looked him in the eye then, and understood. He left.

'Well, Mr Emsworth with your knowledge we would be happy to offer you a place. What makes one of your age come to teaching though. A far more lucrative career would surely be in practice? Not that its always about the money of course.' The man across the desk hastened to add.

'No. It isn't. I was burnt out. Working day and night to keep the employers happy. I just wanted a change of pace.'

'Well, you will certainly get that here. As we are such a small college the students do get a bit more attention from the tutors. I think you will do nicely.'

Eighteen months later, when Mike was on his forth complaint from the female students, the Board thought rather differently.

'Even if they do take you "the wrong way" we still have to be seen to do something. You need to change your approach to the students from now on. We will give you a reference at the end of term if you can show you have changed but you cannot stay here next year. Start looking.' The man stood to signal he was dismissed. 'That's all.'

'Two years at Sedland College. So, you got one lot of students through their A-levels then. Why do you want to leave?'

'I need more of a challenge. More of a higher level of Law. The real stuff. I was a very successful solicitor you know.' Mike puffed out his chest.

It soon deflated at the interviewers next words.
'We gather there was an, "issue" at your last placing-,''

'I thought-,' stammered Mike.

'Oh, it's not on any record.' He gave Mike a sly smile. 'I just happen to know Martine, we go way back. Uni together all those years ago. Stayed in touch.' He stretched his smile to look like the Cheshire cat. 'So, we would be prepared to offer you a place, based on your credentials, but, and this is a BIG but, the first and slightest hint of *any* impropriety or complaints, and I mean any, and we may have to involve the authorities. Do I make myself clear?'

Mike's nod was slight.

'Good. Welcome to the team then.' All hint of earlier distaste now hidden.

He had been really careful. He had even tried paying for it. Just the once and that had not been to his taste at all. Oh no. He had discovered he liked the long game. Test the waters, some had passed the test, some he had to pass up himself. They threw themselves at him, it was laughable really, he was the one saying all the right things, "it's not allowed", he "was old enough to be their father" or, "maybe just this time as you are really my type, but we have to tell no one, I could lose my job we'd never be able to see each other again!" When he tired of them, he pulled out the, "my wife and I… she wants to try again, I do at least owe her that", or "my wife has made an amazing recovery! You do understand don't you." Of *course* they did. No one knew his "wife" was just a fiction, "I like to keep work and home apart", or, "we have separate lives mostly" The photo he used he had cut out of a magazine years ago. He had become quite fond of his fictitious wife. Just the one close call in the last few years and that had been easily rectified. He had dropped her marks back to normal and received some sympathy as he explained to the teacher that she had complained to, she was probably just disgruntled about that, she hadn't put in the same standard of work he assured them when they had asked for, "a quiet word". Fortunately, old Beaton had retired so, it appeared, no one else knew of his past. This one had taken him at his word and, after a few words in the girls' ear, he had upped her marks again, a little, so she passed, just. It had been close, but she was long gone now.

The chill of the cooling bath water bought him came back to the present. It had been a while but with Sophie, there was something about her, something alive and vibrant, besides her hair. That made him smile. She currently had bright pink stars all down the back of it. she was obviously going through that hippy chick or grunge look that most of them had at some point, gender neutral was the fashionable term now wasn't it? Sloppy and unattractive he called it but you could tell, under the baggy clothes there was definitely a body he wanted to find, play with and generally defile, given time, and patience, both of which he had plenty of. He turned on the hot tap, sighed and lay back in his bath.

One year, one bloody long year, but as he stared at himself in the mirror, tonight it would finally be worth the wait. He had *never* waited this long. In fact, at various times he had almost given up or just taken her there in his office. Yes, it had been a close call on occasion but at least he knew she was gagging for it now. It was him who had to put a stop to it last time and it had been really bloody hard and not just the stopping he thought, with a wry smile, God, some nights he had to do it his car! Nearly got caught once. Still, tonight his heaven had arrived on earth. Telling himself not to drink too much, he was pleased he'd had a quickie now, so he didn't rush it later. He was going to take *all* night. The hotel was booked. Champagne in the room, flowers too, everything he could do to make her feel special. Just so she would be grateful enough to want to please him. He couldn't wait, he paced the room. What was the matter with him, she was just another girl wasn't she? He had to admit though he *did* feel especially connected to this one for some reason he couldn't quite explain. Probably just the waiting. He looked at the clock. Time to go. He was *not* going to be late for the best night of his life.

Chapter Twenty-Nine

'You've done WHAT!' His face was contorted in anger but it quickly came back under control when he saw the tears. Last night had fulfilled his wildest dreams and he *definitely* wanted more of that. A LOT more. But this? This could ruin him!

'I just…' sniff '…just wanted to share it, us…with everyone. Last night was so, perfect. I just-' She wiped her nose with her sleeve. It was not a pretty look.

'Last night was *private*.' He snapped.

'I know but us…you and me?' Sophie squirmed.

'There is no-' he stopped he was tempted to say there is no you and me. But he stopped himself. He really did want a bit more of her first. 'There is no reason why everyone else has to know.' He stroked her hair, her face, wiped the tears and kissed her, 'It's so nice, just us two, our little secret, he slid his arm round her back, pulled her close, casually slipped his hand under her jumper. A slight resistance but then, as he stroked her gently, she yielded and he knew he had her. He slid her down the couch and kissed her again. 'Oh, Sophie, oh…my…baby.'

Half an hour later a tidier Sophie was sitting at his desk taking down the posted photo of the two of them. Fortunately, being Sunday none of her campus friends were up yet, so no-one would be any the wiser.

Chapter Thirty

Jess stared at the picture in front of her it was clear as day. The man in the photo, with his arm around her daughter, *was* Michael Emsworth! How on earth had she not seen it before? That dark hair, the smooth, easy going smile? Her phone pinged.

'Have you seen it?!' A frantic Andy must be up and about early. He currently lived somewhere in the Maldives and they were about six hours behind the UK. Scrub *that* thought, he probably hadn't *gone* to bed yet. It was she looked at the time, it was eight o'clock here.

Before she had time to reply it rang.

'It's him! Of all the bloody… It IS him! What is she doing with that BASTARD.' He could still manage to shout even at that early hour.

'She doesn't know, who he is, about it, does she. I know *we* all thought he was her father but she knows nothing and even we aren't.' She chose her words carefully. 'Certain. Are we?'

'We'll have to do something. I'll do something, say something.' He was really agitated now.

'You can't.'

'Why not?'

Jess took a deep breath.

'So, what you're saying is Sophie thinks I'm, what a lech? Grooming her?' Andy was horrified.

'Not, not *exactly*.' She crossed her fingers. That was exactly what Sophie thought.

'But. But she…she's.'

Jess could hear the choke in Andy's voice.

'I know. It's okay.'

'No. It bloody well isn't *OK*'

'It will be okay.' Jess said, not having the foggiest idea how.

'But, this… with Mike, this needs sorting. Like yesterday! Have you *seen* it?'

'Of *course* I-' Jess tried.

Andy ploughed on regardless. '"I have found the love of my life. The true one." For fucks sake.'

'That's not really the point though is it?'

'I Bloody well know *that*! You have to tell her. All of it.' Andy was firm.

'What!' Jess thought he wasn't thinking straight

'Just tell her…it is a… possibility. No tell her you'll get him thrown out. That should do it.'

Jess, who never swore, replied, 'For fucks sake, NO. What do I say? Hi Sophie, good grades, by the way we think your new boyfriend-'

'I'm coming home.'

The line went dead.

'I bloody knew you'd react like this!' Sophie screamed down the phone at her mother.

'SOPHIE! He is your tutor, he has a responsibility.'

'For gods' sake Mum! I'm not at school now, as you are *so fond* of telling me!'

'It is still…immoral.'

'Oh, that is just *so* last year Mum!'

'Andy says-,' Jess realised the error of this before she even finished saying it.

'Andy! What the hell has it got to do with him! Bloody jealous, is he?' Sophie spat.

'You can think what you like but Andy cares about you, and me,' she added quickly, 'we are his family and he...he likes to know we are...alright.' Jess tailed off. She was worried if she continued this conversation, she might blurt out too much.

'I don't bloody well care!' She hung up.

'You will though.' Jess said, to the empty room.

Jess got off the train and headed for the nearest café. She needed to tidy herself up first, she had blood on her sleeve from her finger. It was bleeding again, cut by the roses she had been arranging last night, and steady her nerves. She was relieved when Andy had calmed down and gone to his retreat as planned. Moving to his new flat seemed to have taken his mind off things a bit too. Funny he hadn't mentioned it, though he insisted he had. The landlord was getting married and wanted the whole place back so the three renters had been given their notice along with an invite to the wedding. She was sure she would have remembered *that*. But work had been busy and now she was dating Justin properly some things *did* slip by her. His new place was smaller but she could see the sea out the huge window behind him as he skyped, it was a lovely view always sunny and never any wind, despite being on the coast, the tree in the distance was always perfectly still and, pleasingly, she noticed he seemed happy, distracted, but settled.

Justin made her happy. Happier than she could ever remember being before. He knew about Lucy and she had told him about Amy, he was so sympathetic, she couldn't tell him all of it though, so he still thought Sophie was hers. She had talked about growing up on the farm, her marriage, everything she could, but she still had to keep secrets and now? there was no way he could know about *this*. Love him, he thought she was in town talking to a flower supplier about a job. She really hated deceiving him. Especially as she knew he would understand. But it wasn't her secret to tell, even with Amy gone. What she was going to say to Mike when she saw *him*, she had no idea. She wasn't even sure he would know who she was after all this time.

'Come in.' Mike answered the knock. Bending over the desk, rummaging through a pile of paper and books, he stared at the figure in front of him. Not quite sure what to make of the visitor; long, curly, red hair, the high heels, tanned face. 'Do I, um, know you?' He was squinting now, had stopped playing with the books on the desk.

'You should.' The scarlet lips replied.

The husky voice, it was a bit familiar, a parent? An old client, colleague? 'Sorry, I can't quite place…' He came around the desk and held out his hand, a friendly, slightly puzzled smile, frowned on his own face.

'We need to talk,' almost a whisper, 'about Sophie.' A broad smile stretched across the unplaceable face.

Mike was confused now, the grip was firm, too firm, all of a sudden…he was on the floor, winded, when he tried to get up, he couldn't, then a scarf was stuffed in his mouth. He didn't see the blade but he felt the pain hit him and he grabbed his side. His hand felt wet, warm, sticky? he held it up, blood ran down his arm, staining his cuff, he tried again to move but the figure on him was strong, heavier than it looked, the long hair brushed his face as he heard the voice close to his ear...

'You should have known this was coming, that one day I would be coming for you...just like the other three? But now this has bought things to a head don't you think?'

The voice was fading now, or was it him fading away? Incense? what the hell... incense... he looked at the hair, what was strange about it? Realisation set in as he slipped, quietly, away.

The visitor, satisfied the man on the floor was dead, stood up and, after some rummaging, made to look like a burglary, they picked up the rucksack and slipped out, unseen.

As Sophie pushed opened the door a voice shouted. 'Get help. NOW.'

Seeing Mike on the floor with a figure bent over him, Sophie went to scream.

'I just came in and found him like this, he needs help.' The woman on the floor said, breathlessly, as she looked round her eyes widened. 'Sophie!'

'MUM! What did you do?' Sophie pulled out her phone and rang 999. She bent over and cradled Mike's head. 'I know you didn't like him, but this!'

'Sophie you have to believe me! I found him like it.' But Sophie, realising he was dead, was rocking back and forth crying and wailing for her lost love.

Chapter Thirty-One

'I opened the door and saw him on the floor, I had just bent down to check for a pulse when my daughter opened the door.' Jess tried to keep calm.

'But you said you didn't know who opened the door.' The DI quickly jumped on the statement.

'Inspector, my client has been over this time and again, she didn't know, when it opened, who it was but now she does. She is tired and it was just a slip of the tongue.'

'We are all tired Mr Styles but we at least all get to wake up again, Mr Emsworth won't. Will he?' The policeman stared hard at Jess.

'Look, you have no murder weapon, nothing but circumstantial evidence. Charge my client or let her go.' Mr Styles sounded bored now.

'We have a lot of motive and if they were in it together.' He left the rest unsaid.

'NO!' Jess screeched.

Mr Styles patted her hand. 'It's alright my dear.' he reassured her.

'If they were in it together, the murder weapon could have been disposed of by Sophie.' He concluded and sat back. 'Come.' A young PC entered the room and handed him a piece of paper.

'Well, well, looks like we have the murder weapon, and what's the betting we find your fingerprints all over it.' He pulled a smug smile

Jess shot a worried look at Mr Styles 'They won't, they can't. Please.' She looked at the tired looking man as he sat fiddling with his nails opposite her. 'Please, we *didn't* do this.' The policeman stood and left. He slammed the door shut behind him.

The solicitor stood up and began to fill his briefcase. 'I think you had better get used to being here, at least for now,' he patted her shoulder and, with reassurance he didn't feel, added, 'we will know more tomorrow.' He tried to keep a neutral face. He was not so sure of her now.

'Sophie, how... where is my daughter?'

'Ah. She has a separate council. I will see what I can find out. But rest for now, I think you may have a long night.'

'I already told you. I came in to see Mi...Erm...Mr Emsworth about something and found someone leaning over him. When she turned I saw that it was my mum! I was so shocked by her and him I just-,'

'Sorry, Sophie, her and him, you mean you caught them...together?'

'What. NO. I found her on the floor over Mike's-,' she swallowed, '-Mr Emsworths' body.'

'Did you Sophie? could it not be that you found them...together... and in a jealous rage-,'

Sophie looked mortified, how could they know what she had thought?

'In a jealous rage, you took it out on him and now your mum is covering for you? Isn't that what happened.

We have the weapon Sophie, we will know soon enough.'

'Can I see my mum?' Asked a shrunken Sophie, the fight had left her voice now.

'Not gonna happen.' She pushed the chair back and terminated the interview.

'What, what now?' Sophie burst into tears and sobbed. 'I just want my mum.'

Zoe looked at her client, torn over whether or not she believed her.

The policewoman just shook her head and carried on out the door. They had checked the CCTV, the only people on it were Jess, Sophie and a cleaner, they were trying, not too hard, to trace.

The next morning the headlines were screaming about the mother, daughter, tutor, murder triangle.

Andy knew a long stay in the spa would restore his energy, they worked you very hard here and took your phone, and any other techno gadgets. Here it was just you, the trees and the exercise. It would be another month before he got them back.

When they returned his phone, he saw 137 emails in his box, not bad actually, he clicked on news at home, then news in England. Andy read the news item over and over again. Head in hands. The timing was unbelievable, how could that even be possible! He knew though. This time he knew he had to be there. To help save the girls. How could anyone possibly believe that the two women pictured here had done what they were saying. He had to make them listen. Make someone listen. He scrolled through his contacts until he found what he needed.

Mike's dad sat, head in hands, at the news. No tears shed but his brow was wet with perspiration, he wiped his hand across his face, not caring that the cuffs of his crisp white Armani shirt were now grimy from it. Truth be told though he always suspected his son might come to a bad end. He had heard the rumours, that probably *weren't* just rumours. The conversation with Amy's dad when he'd bumped into him whilst in the village to finalise the house sale, he knew he had been really unpleasant to him but, honestly? Had he really thought it was that unlikely? After Dan had confronted him, he *had* partly believed that Dan may be exacting revenge, when he heard of the deaths of two other boys involved. He sighed, knowing that *his* apple hadn't fallen too far from the tree did it? He *had* meant to apologise to Lucy but then decided to leave the past where it was, after all they had both moved on, hadn't they? had happy marriages and families. No, best let sleeping dogs lie. Coward… screamed his inner mind, but he had learned long ago not to listen to *that*. He would ID the body, do his duty, then return pronto to Hong Kong.

'Yes,' he sighed, 'that is my son.' He spoke to the police officer but his eyes stayed on the sleeping shape of his heir in front of him. His hopes for the boy when he was born flashed across his mind; he would grow up and be a partner to his father, he would marry and produce another heir, to continue the family firm so when he retired the, "and son", would remain intact. He had killed that idea though when his son turned out to be lousy with figures. Except the female kind.

Chapter Thirty-Two

The two women sat next to each other in the wooden and glass container, both wearing smart navy trouser suits. Jess with a lilac blouse, Sophie in a pale pink vest. They had each aged by at least 10 years and they glanced at each other, fear on both faces. Jess went to touch her daughter but the guard put out a hand and shook her head, a tired but smug look on her face. They both knew the evidence wasn't looking good for them. It was Jess's blood found on the knife, she couldn't fathom how, so Sophie was being charged as an accessory, the belief being she got rid of the weapon. They had both been urged to plead guilty but neither of them would. They *weren't*, they each stressed to their counsel, so how could they be expected to say they were. Jess looked across the room and was mortified to see Justin. She had refused to allow him to visit and had had no contact with him since her arrest. Next to him was his sister, Lizzie, Jess's closest friend. Mona and her daughter had made the trip to be there for them, but the last she heard of her son he was out in some remote island off Malaysia, she hadn't even been able to get him on skype when this started. Lena was whispering something to her mum. Jess also knew Mona had been seeing Lucy daily as the end was quite near, but Mona didn't change her expression. She had hoped to be out to see her mum before she died but now? The reality was hitting her and she had her first wave of doubt. Tears filled her eyes and she wiped them away. The day was only just beginning.

The police and the forensic specialist gave evidence, how the blood was a match, there were some uncommon markers, steroids mainly, but yes, *he* was certain, definitely Jess and no, no they couldn't be mistaken, of course not, they ran a tight ship yada, yada, yada. The fingerprints were not clear but they matched several points, Jess couldn't understand what they were talking about but the jury seemed impressed. She was worried. As the prosecutor finished addressing the jury the courtroom had fallen silent and, in the pause, the sound of footsteps, clicking down the hall, getting louder, closer, could be heard. When they stopped all heads turned to the door as the handle moved and the door creaked opened…

    Jess could not *believe* what she was seeing.

    Sophie was *unsure* what she was seeing. The figure *looked* familiar but, something was off. She looked at her mum, puzzled, she was crying and smiling at the same time. What the fuck! It was Uncle Andy! And he was dressed as a bloody woman, now that really *was* sick. More to the point what was he doing here? They hadn't heard from him since the day…the day Mike was killed.

    'Oh God, Oh. My. God.' Sophie's hands flew to her face. The figure, the figure that had passed her in the gardens when she came in, she had tried to tell them…no one had believed her. But the blood? Her *mums* blood on the murder weapon…They watched as the piece of paper, held out in the hand of the visitant, was passed to the clerk of the court, who, in turn, gave it to the Judge. After reading it she stared, open mouthed at the figure in her courtroom, she quickly recovered and called over the police officer in attendance who, after a hurried whispering, removed his handcuffs from his belt and walked towards Andy. He held out his hands without protest. Both the legal representatives were beckoned to the Judges podium and, after some hasty discussion, pointing and general hand waving, they returned to collect their papers. Both stared at the handcuffed prisoner and hurried out. The Judge called for a recess. The women looked at each other but, were unable to converse as they were led away in different directions.

'So, what you are saying, let me just…just get this straight in my head.' Sophie threw her hands up in the air warning off the concerned solicitor. 'So, what you are saying is…we will be free to go?'
'Well there are a few ends to tie up, but yes, you and your, erm, mother are to be excused.' Sophie sank to the floor.

Several weeks later both women sat side by side in the courtroom again. This time in the gallery. In the glass container sat a solitary figure. As they were walked to the podium their eyes locked with Jess. A faint smile and a glance at Sophie. Then the hand was raised and, voice wavering, they began.

'I am now known as Andy Collier and I killed Michael Emsworth. He was one of my childhood friends and also one of my,' the words stopped, he took a deep breath and carried on, 'rapists, as a teenager and… the…the father of my daughter, Sophie, whom he groomed,' the eyes lifted upwards, 'yes, he did,' the voice whispered, then, much clearer, 'and then took as a lover.' The speaker looked again at the girl in the gallery. Sophie was now weeping silent tears, Jess wiped them away and hugged her close. One day Sophie would realise that she had been lucky enough to have had more than one mother who loved her very, very much.

Just not yet.

After several long and varied examinations, it was jointly agreed that, at the time of the murder of Mike Emsworth the accused had been suffering from a mental condition due to the initial trauma and, quite probably something similar to post-natal depression, none of which had been addressed when his sex change operation was performed. Depression was considered a usual side effect during the wait so treatment at a secure facility was the recommended sentence including the death of Tony Hodder, strange how both brothers died by drowning, and Dave Camber, hit by Amy's bike, before it hit the wall, they were still arguing whether or not that was an accident. The question still remained of Stuart Hodder, the hit and run she was guilty but on the beach, having been alive, then left, before calling for help? If they wanted to add that to the others, so be it. A confinement sentence was inevitable whatever so it would make no difference now. Now they just had to wait for a place in the right institution and one where

Jess and hopefully, given time, Sophie could visit easily. It had been a lot for her to take in but she had resumed her studies and was immersing herself in that for the moment.

Jess had tried to explain to Lucy about Andy but after the first few words she gave up. She was in a coma now, not much longer the doctor had said. They had tried to get a visit for Andy before the end but, due to the technicalities involved it was too late. Lucy's funeral was a small affair, a couple of people from the home, an old childhood friend, Jess and Sophie. Andy was brought, accompanied and a little medicated, but at least he was able to say goodbye. Mona hugged him tight. Both her children came too before Luke went back to Bali where he had joined his dad. Phil had mellowed these days, a close call helped him give up the free spirit lifestyle, as they termed his extreme drinking, he'd settled with a local girl, so at least someone was looking out for him *and* keeping him off the booze. Luke liked the weather out there and was teaching scuba diving. Mona had hoped he might come home one day but he was happy and that is all she could ask right now. Jess noticed John Banstead, the carpenter, at the back and caught the look that passed between him and Mona. Well I never! Good for her. Jess smiled to herself as she considered it was about time Mona had something to *not* moan about. She turned back to look at Justin and ran her hand over the tiny bump. Maybe, just maybe, now was time for their family to have a happy story.

WIGHT GOLD

Available now on Amazon

Sgt. Archie Etherington currently has a nice cosy life. Living in a little cottage on his family's estate in the New Forest. After many years undercover he now spends his time chasing sheep and eating biscuits! However, life is about to change. Big time!

He is being promoted! With responsibility! And, even worse…It's ABROAD! He consoles himself with the fact that, 'they don't have any actual *crime* on the Isle of Wight, do they?!'

Chapter One

'OW!' Archie, disturbed by the tugging at his ankle, connected his head with the bonnet and found his black Labrador puppy at his feet. Bertie was bored now and waiting for a game. It was Sunday, he expected a wander by the pond or at least a ball game! Archie rubbed a gloved, greasy hand through his chestnut hair and felt a small bump. At least *she* doesn't mind where she's going, he thought as he slammed the bonnet of his car, female of course, and pulled out a rag from his pocket. This action pleased the little dog no end as it flicked out some doggy chocs with it. He went off in search of them all, his tiny nose hoovering the floor. Archie peeled off the latex gloves and threw them in the makeshift bin in the corner of his lean-to carport. His real garage was home to his classic car project and, after tea, with the accompanying biccies, and a ball game he would try to fit a restored panel. Then he saw the oil and cobweb covered dog appear from under the work bench and smiled.

'You can't keep out of trouble for 5 minutes! Can you?' He said to little dog, who was managing a good job of totally ignoring him!

Inside the little brick cottage on his family's New Forest estate, Archie stood at the white butler sink, currently filling with bubbles, with a lukewarm mug of tea in his hand that proclaimed; 'a Policeman's plot is a very happy one,' with a picture of three happy, smiley carrots underneath it. At least he'd *thought* they were carrots until a gardening colleague had pointed out that, "yes, the orange one *was* a carrot but its friends? Well, the white one's a parsnip and the little round purple one? That's actually a beetroot!" Never mind, green fingered he wasn't! He looked out the wooden sash window and, with the leaves now down, he could clearly make out the top windows of the old, solid stone family house in the distance and wondered if his brother, Parker and their father, "Lordy" were up yet. He had to smile to himself at the nickname. It had been given to him by his grandchildren. Archie and his siblings would never have got away with calling him *that*! but Lord Etherington-Smythe doted on his daughter's twins.

He was going to miss this view, he thought with harsh realization, then he felt sick at the thought of:

a) Leaving!

b) Responsibility!

Now there were a few things Archie didn't 'do'. Patience, domestic chores, and as for decorating, he looked at the wide brush marks in the paint on the walls of the cottage. He really *had* thought it would be quicker to just whitewash with a broom! But the first two things were right up there on the list of what to avoid in life, along with boiling your head and clamping your hand in a vice. Though the latter he had actually managed to do. Just the once.

He knew his work record had kept him fairly safe from disturbance. He had been undercover for almost 10 years. By a pure fluke when he had first joined up he had overheard a conversation and, having been a brilliant actor, he couldn't resist the challenge. He had cajoled and let's be honest he thought, pulled a few *more* strings, and throughout his years of undercover work he had been responsible for so much information he had had to give up in the end for his own safety, not that anyone else knew that. These days he just didn't want any responsibility. *Really* at 38? His Chief, however, had other ideas. Archie had passed, with flying colours, his Inspectors exams some time, alright years, before but, due to his total reluctance to leave home again, he did not have a posting. Now, though, he was being sent away to cover for a sick colleague. He could still hear the Chiefs words - "Who knows, you might even enjoy it." And, to make matters even worse, it was ABROAD!

He recalled his friend and neighbour Mrs Beamish considered that the Isle of Wight, known to locals as 'The Island,' was definitely abroad. "Can I get there without getting my feet wet? Thought not. I rest my case!" And that was, always, the end of the conversation. His own opinion being that 10 miles was far enough these days.

Returned back to the present by the scratch-scratch, scratch-scratch, on the old wooden door, that was getting louder and more frantic, he went to turn off the tap. In his absence soapy water had poured over the edge and soaked his feet, trousers and the quarry tiled floor. Bertie was getting desperate now, pawing and whining, just when he was tired, he was being kept away from his bed *and* the tin – the one where, despite his young age, he already knew the doggy sweets were kept! Archie checked for a couple of towels and went to let the dirty little dog inside.

That afternoon, Archie sat on the back step of his little cottage and tickled the tummy of the three-month old black Labrador at his feet, his little legs wriggling around with joy. The *puppy's* not Archie's!

'Sorry, Bertie my little time-waster I know you only just got here but I have to go away for a bit. You will be perfectly fine with Mrs Beamish to look after you.' He looked carefully at the wrinkled little face, as if willing him to understand, but Bertie had seen a butterfly to chase and ran off.

Archie's main worry was, in fact, that he would come back to a puppy that looked like a little barrel, his neighbour's motto: "Feed 'em up and slow 'em down," apparently applied equally well to dogs as to children! He had seen many skinny waifs fill out under her care....and cakes. But, despite regularly feeding *him* with her home-baked pies, cakes and biscuits he remained stick thin, he was perfectly fit, just spare, and although he was excellent at sport, his interest only extended to teaching his niece and nephew tennis in the summer, after all someone had to make use of the courts, personally he much preferred a peaceful wander round the estate with some canine company.

The little dog soon bundled his way back to Archie. 'Phwoar.' His nose wrinkled and his eyes watered as the familiar smell assaulted his nostrils. 'Mrs B, Have you any..?' He started to shout when a small plastic packet, perfectly aimed, landed at his feet, thrown over the low rail, covered by Clematis, that separated the two back gardens. On seeing the wet wipes Archie felt the furry little bundle instinctively make a run for it...straight towards the lounge door, where his neatly packed suitcase lay open…

'Noooo!' He shouted as he spun round and scrambled to his feet. The image that flashed across his mind of arriving at his new appointment covered in au de Reynard was just too much!

'Come back! You little monkey.' Archie set off after the speedy little black mass. Bertie, sensing a chase coming on, ran around in circles and yapped happily at the game that, in his mind at least, his master was now playing. He then bounced up on to the brown leather sofa... and straight into the open case!

'Don't you dare! Not my clean clothes... Come back here...!' His voice getting more and more desperate as he watched him disappear out of the door complete with clean socks in his mouth! Archie sensed his day was going to get worse. SPLASH... Oh, yes... It just got worse! The hole in Mrs B's fence still waiting for repair, really must remember to speak to my brother about that *again*, he thought, had allowed Bertie to slip through… straight into the small, weed covered pond at the end of the long garden next door.

'Quack, quack, quack.' Several disgruntled Aylesbury ducks scattered to the far corners as Mrs B's head appeared above the fence, having been in the process of evicting one small duck from under her kitchen table. This was not unusual as the crumbs always on the floor from her many cooking sessions ensured an "open door" policy where the fowl were concerned, and most of the village come to that!

'I think there is something belonging to you over here, still at least it won't require the wet wipes now, just a towel.' Mrs B, looking, as usual, like she had just stepped out of a Damart catalogue, in her smart tracksuit, reached down and smartly grabbed the furball as he whizzed past. 'Years of practice, with small children.' She told him as she passed the cosy bundle, now wrapped in a fluffy towel, back over to his owner.

'Thank you.' He looked at Bertie with what he hoped was a suitably cross face! Grasping him tightly he rubbed at him and put him down, where he then proceeded to go and roll in the gardens gold coloured dust! Now he looked like he should be in a toilet tissue advert!

'Why are you not packing. I thought you had an early start?' She asked, knowing how disorganised he was.

'Done.' He said rather smugly. 'Alarm set for ten to seven, should be in time for the nine o'clock sailing.' He knew he sounded rather unenthusiastic, he detested personal change and disruptions to his routine. He refused many a promotion as it would mean leaving his safe, cosy existence. It wasn't exactly laziness... just...actually ...it probably *was* just laziness!

'Got your seasick pills handy?' His surrogate mum asked, breaking through his daydreams.

Honestly that was too much!

'Mrs Beamish just because I was sick ONCE... just the once, when I was about 10 years old, does NOT make me seasick!' he sounded cross, but it was just worry.

'Can't be too careful. Have a safe trip and call me when you get there. OK?' Archie felt the "can I get there without getting my feet wet?" conversation on the way but was saved by the scrunch of tyres on gravel, they both looked round as a car sped down the lane. In a cloud of dust, a dark blue, now very much in need of a wash, Jaguar skidded to a halt, just missing the gate post as it pulled up.

'Oh, no.' Mrs B. slapped on her best fake smile. The driver poured herself out of the vehicle wearing a top and jeans that she must have sprayed on that morning, or maybe last night, she thought wickedly, looking at the mussy, long blonde hair and the not quite so perfect make-up - the ridiculously high heels gave nothing away though, day or night, she was never out of them.

'Archie, *Dharling*, so glad to catch you.... LOOOK!' Petronella Carmichael waved her left hand around and nearly blinded the pair of them with the glint from the mountainous diamond on it.

'My goodness, you could down a plane with the ray from that!' Mrs B watched Archie VERY closely for his reaction to this news. Secretly she was pleased, really, really pleased.

'Well, well Petrol, you've snagged number... four, is it? I struggle to keep up.' Giving nothing away, Archie thought and today is *still* getting worse by the minute.

Archie and "Petrol Head", so called from her love of all things wheeled and fast, (this had included Hubby no 2, affectionately known as "Wheelchair Walter"), had known each other since childhood and he had of late, well actually since the departure, to pastures younger, of Hubby number three, spent many a late evening as her companion to all the glittery balls she "couldn't possibly attend unaccompanied and, of course, you know all the right people *dharling*."

Technically, they were well suited he knew but, if he was honest, he found her a little scary! And who fell in love due to technicalities anyway. Still, his sister, Fiona, would be a little disappointed, she thought of Petrol as very suitable material for him, despite her many husbands, "after all, what's a little mileage here and there you, of all people, wouldn't pass up a classic car now, would you? She's had the practice rounds", Fiona compared *everything* to her horses, "now she's ready for the main event". Yes, he remembered, she had actually said that!

'What a good job you'll have company then as Archie won't be back for some time.' Interjected Mrs B. 'So, who's the latest idiot...I mean lucky chap then?' The sarcasm, as always, failed to hit the spot.

'Humphrey Rivington-Sharpe!' Petronella replied as she gave a little squeal, jumped up and down on the spot and clapped her hands together in a strange little "lucky me" type gesture.

'Humph! He must be twice your age?' Archie was stupefied.

'I know, but at last I'll be LADY Petronella, isn't it just so.... just. I can't wait to tell Miranda Pennington... she'll be *so* jealous. Buy a new hat Mrs Beamish, you can't possibly wear the one you've worn to the last three.' This was not sarcasm, just the world according to the fashion conscious.

'There is nothi...' Mrs B decided to stop there, it probably *was* time for a new hat, maybe wedding outfit altogether as her floaty, cerise ensemble really *should* be updated. Let's face it, she realised, the entire village could hold its own version of "Where's Wally" in their wedding albums at this rate! No, best take a trip to Salisbury or perhaps Southampton...*very* soon.

'Safe, safe Archie, cheery bye-bye.' Petronella's voice bought her back to the here and now.

They both watched as, narrowly avoiding a curious chicken that had been foolish enough to wander under her car, Petronella, soon to be Lady, shot off, wheels spinning and car askew.

'She wasn't right for you Archie, you do see that don't you?' Concern was on her face as she peered at him, little realising that it was driving Petronella's car he would miss the most, as she wouldn't be seen dead in his "old banger." Actually, it *was* old, but the Saab that used to be his mothers, was in pristine condition. He continued to lavish attention on it, in her memory.

'C'mon little fella.' Archie threw the ball and, waving to Mrs Beamish, he wandered off for a stroll round the woods.

j

Archie was woken at about 2am by a loud crashing noise and his first thought was 'hooray the ferry will be cancelled!' As he climbed out of his cosy, warm bed he could hear Bertie whining downstairs. He must be scared of the storm, 'I'm coming, I'm coming,' he passed the window just as the lightning put on an impressive show and lit up the room, then his face dropped in horror, the source of the noise hadn't been the little dog knocking something over downstairs but the ancient oak tree which gave the two cottages their name that was now lying horizontal... right across his polished blue Saab!

He ran downstairs, missing most of them, not quite sure what he was going to do and then he heard Mrs B knocking on the wall and knew he'd have to go and check she was ok. Fortunately, they still had the electric and two cups of cocoa and a game of pass the parcel, with the blanket wrapped Bertie later, they said their goodnights as the storm was now over and went to their respective beds, having decided that Archie would call a taxi in the morning, as the ferries would be running now, and his car would have to go through the insurance, having been virtually cut in half! He'd also ring Parker to take care of the tree. They'd be kept in firewood for months! He was sad to see the magnificent tree gone though.

'TOOT, TOOT.' It was the taxi. Outside Mrs B was waiting to take his key and, after collecting his cases, he nuzzled Bertie then a miserable Archie climbed into the taxi. He gave a little wave as it drove away.

'C'mon Bertie,' she looked at the forlorn little furball, who brightened considerably at her next words, 'there's some cheese in the fridge and I think I'm going to enjoy dog share.' He obviously knew the word fridge as she found him sitting by it! She would soon learn that he knew 'sweets' and 'dinner' too but 'sit' or 'wait' appeared to be *way* beyond him!

The taxi arrived in plenty of time for his crossing so Archie went into the coffee bar at the terminus. Decorated in red leather and wooden panels he approached the counter and was met with the usual array of plastic food, designed to make you feel at home no matter wherever you happened to be, same look, same taste...hmm... He picked a breakfast croissant with an orange juice and was already missing Mrs B's culinary skills. He found a booth but after just couple of bites he rose from the booth and balled his rubbish, helpfully taking it to the bin, it wasn't busy but old boarding school habits die hard. Collecting his luggage, he exited the glass doors and headed for the ferry.

Sea, sea and more sea! Archie stared out of the window from his seat in the middle of the ship (to avoid the sea-sickness which he didn't suffer from!) Was it still a window on a ship? Ferry? Did it really matter? Feeling very sorry for himself, and more than a little queasy now, he picked up a discarded copy of the County Press and pretended to look interested in it while his mind drifted... let's face it, he thought, Petronella was just destined to keep making bad marriages... and lots of money! Still, they would always remain friends.

She was the sister of an old friend from the village but Seb had never understood when Archie "ran off" from his privileged upbringing. He was sociable when they met, but they'd lost their boyhood closeness. He still missed it. A broken voice over the tannoy cut through his thoughts.

'We will soon be docking in Yarmouth, could passengers make sure they have all their belongings.'

He stood and collected his baggage; one carrier bag, containing wellingtons, a small, black holdall and a khaki wheeled bag. He didn't plan on being there for long. As he replaced the paper he caught sight of the date and his chest tightened as he realised it was nearly another awful anniversary. He sighed and pushed away the memory as he joined the passengers as they headed for the disembarking point and stood watching the tree covered land get bigger and the two visible church spires get taller, before disappearing altogether. The feeling of being "abroad" growing ever stronger.

As Archie walked towards the dock in the cool sunshine, a complete contrast to the previous night's storm, he could taste the salt in the air that somehow seemed stronger this side of the crossing. He looked around and was surprised to see a police car, lights ablaze with a uniformed driver standing beside it. Briefly wondering who the criminal was to get this reception, he did a quick scan of the other passengers, looking for anything that could be deemed as suspicious behaviour, he was somewhat perturbed when the PC approached him.

'D.I Etherington?' Asked the uniform, as he extended a hand. 'I am P.C Bobble.'

'But I was just expecting a taxi?' Archie said puzzled 'And it's *Acting* D.I…Bobble... was it?' He asked, unsure if he had heard right. 'I'm only here 'til D.I Blake is better so please, just Archie is fine.'

'Ookay... *Acting* D.I.Etherrington,' Bobble tried again, 'I am sorry Sir, but we have a body.... I am here to take you straight to the crime scene!'

Coming to Amazon in 2019

TEA BREAK TALES.

A collection on Kindle of short women magazine style tales.

WIGHT LIES.

The second instalment of the new Wight series.

Blake is due back at work, sick leave over, but a sudden death changes the team dynamic and, unexpectedly, throws up an awful lot of suspects.

Coming in 2020

CAN'T CATCH ME.

A policeman and a social worker, the perfect pairing for foster parents. And cover ups. Crime, it seems, *does* pay.

Behind closed doors? Just don't let the kids break their rules.

IF I TELL YOU...

'If I tell you, I'd have to kill you.' The girl smiled and, head on side, played with strands of her long blonde hair.

Opposite, Gemma gave a small laugh, sharing the joke.

If you have, I hope, enjoyed this story please leave feedback on Amazon.

Thank you.

If you prefer you can contact me

gdjackman2017@gmail.com

Printed in Great Britain
by Amazon